· Date

Up All Night

Up All Night

Edited by R.P. MacIntyre

THISTLEDOWN PRESS

Canadian Cataloguing in Publication Data

Up all night

ISBN 1-894345-27-4
1. Young adult fiction, Canadian (English).*
2. Short stories, Canadian (English).*
3. Canadian fiction (English)—20th century.*
I. MacIntyre, R.P. (Roderick Peter), 1947–

PS8329.U66 2000   C813'.01089283   C00-920203-X
PR9197.32.U6 2000

Cover photograph by Ian Sanderson/Masterfile
Cover and book design by J. Forrie
Typeset by Thistledown Press Ltd.
Printed and bound in Canada

Thistledown Press Ltd.
633 Main Street
Saskatoon, Saskatchewan, S7H 0J8

 Canadian Patrimoine
Heritage canadien

Thistledown Press gratefully acknowledges the financial assistance of the
Canada Council for the Arts, the Saskatchewan Arts Board, and the
Government of Canada through the Book Publishing Industry Development
Program for its publishing program.

UP ALL NIGHT

Contents

The Piano Lesson

Anne Carter

She climbs the stairs to the third floor of the Conservatory. David, her piano teacher, is waiting for her. He teaches in a large studio with his tabby cat, Tripod, and always wears a T-shirt, covered in cat hair, black jeans and turquoise running shoes. Every few months however, he colours the halo of his hair. Lately it's been green to match his glasses.

She missed last week's lesson and he asks her if she is okay. She lies and is uneasy because of it. He asks her for a C-major scale, the easiest scale on the piano, one she has known since she was six, but he asks for four octaves, top to bottom — he's so contrary! — left hand only. She has never played a scale this way before. It throws her.

"That was fine," he comments. "Good finger action. Too bad it was three octaves. Try the right hand, same thing."

She starts and he interrupts immediately. "No. I want top to bottom."

"I don't play it that way. I always start at the bottom."

"I know. That's the point."

She swears inwardly at him. But she is well brought-up. At least, she used to be. She's feeling brought down since last week.

"Hmm. That was five octaves. I guess that's eight all together. Practise that for me this week, will you. Just the C-major scale. Hands separate. Top to bottom."

The other technical exercises are equally disastrous. He opens up the Chopin nocturne. She loves this piece, wants to play it well. "You've memorized it?" he asks.

"I'm trying. I'm having a little trouble."

"What key is it in?"

David would ask this question. He takes his role seriously. He is the master, she the student. He won't let her relax, drift into la-la land, but demands that she think about the music she is playing, understand its structure. In the year she has studied with him, her playing has improved dramatically. Last spring she received the second highest mark in the provincial exams, and her father, who has paid for another year's tuition, is pleased.

But she hasn't practised for two weeks. Only this morning did she look at the key signature, knowing David would ask his nasty questions at the lesson.

The piece has four sharps in the key signature and is somewhat haunting, in a minor key. She is confident of her answer. "C-sharp minor."

"What's your base note?"

Mouth open, she looks up at the music for help. Too late. He moves in, closes the score, takes it.

"You're in C-sharp minor. What's your base note?"

"C-sharp," she says, staring at a black key on the keyboard. But she's guessing.

"Yes. That's your anchor. Tonic chord, first position."
He stands up and moves the chair well behind her, giving
them some psychological, as well as physical, distance. He
sniffs constantly. He has told her, in confidence, that he has
AIDS, and she wonders if the excess of fluid in his nose is
a symptom. Bodily fluids have a way of being treacherous.

"Now play the first two lines, please. Remember with
Chopin, keep a cantabile melody in the right hand, soft
accompaniment in the left."

She tries to clear her mind. Focus. All fall she's had
trouble memorizing this piece. She's having trouble alright.
Treble trouble. Base trouble. Boy trouble.

Somehow, the first two lines are in her fingers. She stops
thinking, no longer using her brain, and plays from a
different part of her inner being. It's like sex with the boy.
Turning off the brain and responding with the body. She
thinks of the boy. She loves his dark curls and the way he
sits, yoga style, when they talk. They are both eighteen,
both in first-year university, although he lives in South
Carolina where they linger over syllables. In the south they
call it "Caaawww-llege" as if it were a school for hungry
crows.

"Stop." David moves and stands beside her again. "I can
certainly hear the right hand. Only I wouldn't call it
singing." He has a sarcastic tone and a mischievous smile
on his face. "That was rather butch for my taste."

She laughs. David shocks her sometimes by giving
unusual sexual meanings to music. It makes her think
differently. He is outrageous. It's a secret between them.
Her father pays for the lessons and assumes that David is
a proper Conservatory of Music teacher like the ones who
taught her father two generations earlier. She is the

daughter of her father's old age, born when he was over fifty. But she is not keeping him young. In fact, last week, he looked quite old and unwanted, like an aborted grandfather.

No. Her father would definitely be uncomfortable if he overheard David call her playing butch or worse, tell her anecdotes about his dates with truck drivers, engineers, waiters, men from all walks of life and nationalities.

David moves back a few steps, megaphones his hand in front of his mouth. "Music is language. It's communicating. It's the voice of God, of your soul and emotions. Do you really think Chopin meant to say, *Heh, honey, get over here and take your clothes off?*"

She giggles. So does he. Already she feels the depression that has overwhelmed her during the last few weeks lift, like a few wrong notes, latin calypso in the middle of a requiem.

"What does nocturne mean?"

She took Latin for two years in high school. "Something to do with nighttime." She smiles, suddenly anticipating where David will go with this.

"Good answer. Especially, I would think, bedtime activities. So I want this to be delicate. Sensual. As if one fingertip is ever so lightly — " He stops abruptly.

Is there a look on her face? A memory of the boy, last summer, left on her cheekbones?

"Start from the top of page two."

Oh God. Her mind goes completely blank. So do her fingers. She places them on the piano, right thumb on E but . . . what goes with it? What is the chord in the left hand? Her body is letting her down. The memory is not there.

"What key are you in?" David repeats.

"G-sharp major," she says, desperately remembering the lesson from two weeks ago. She knows that G-sharp is the fifth note of the C-sharp minor scale. It has a perfect relationship to C-sharp minor.

"No."

"Okay," she fumbles. "How about G-sharp minor? F-sharp minor? I don't know, David — "

"It's A-major." David cuts her off swiftly. David loves accuracy. He may fool around with lovers, but never, never, with music.

Tripod, David's beloved cat, jumps onto the windowsill. He is a three-legged cat and he barely makes it. He lies on the wide sill, purring. If she plays well, Tripod will jump down and approach her, wrap himself around her calves, rubbing with pleasure. But Tripod is looking lazily out the window, uninterested in her. She takes this as a bad sign.

"A-major?" She is incredulous. What is Chopin doing in A-major? How did this transition happen?

David goes into a mini-lecture on harmony, the relationship of A-major to C-sharp minor. He finds a pencil and prods her, harasses her into analyzing all the changes of key on the second page. There are too many. Her mind is spinning.

He flips up the music holder on the piano and returns the marked-up page so that she can read it. She does not want to analyze. She resents thinking; she wants to let herself go. Somewhere in her mind, she knows she should be examining her life like a piece of music. What if she tells David, her brilliant teacher, her dilemma? Would he force her to examine the fingering and harmony, the rhythm and behaviour of the boy and herself, so that she understands their relationship? Would she know what to do then? Not just with her spirit and her body, but with her brain, so that she could translate their love from top to bottom, in any direction, and know how to play this out?

But that is not why she comes to the studio, is it? She chastises herself: David is just her piano teacher.

She is lonely. She misses the boy. Her mind spins again.

"Divide the page into sections," David lectures. "Play the sections randomly until you know them so intimately, they're in your deep tissue. You can't memorize a piece unless you understand it. Play the third bar in the first line, please."

Deep tissue. She plays the third bar thinking about the size of an unwanted ten-week-old fetus, smaller than her thumb.

"And again."

She plays the bar again, noticing it is in F-sharp minor.

"Good. That was better. Now turn to page three. Let me hear the first bar in the fourth line."

She looks at the third page, takes a deep breath and plays the requested bar. In the first two beats of the first bar in the fourth line, there are thirty-five notes in the right hand against four eighth-notes in the left. She has practised this many times, so many times, she can now, amazingly, do it, though she doesn't know how. It seems a bit like happiness: some days it just happens.

"That was beautiful." David sits beside her and takes her hand, massages it gently. "Relax your hands. Let your wrists be still. Articulate your fingers. You're supported in the back," he places a hand lightly against the small of her back, "in your shoulders, right down to your fingers. You don't throw weight from your shoulders to produce sound; you don't need excessive movement. Good sound comes from a well-articulated finger."

She likes the feel of David's hand against the small of her back. It calms her; something happens inside her when his hand is there. She feels stronger, as if she has a centre that is connected with the universe, as if she could be anything she wanted to be, do anything she wanted to do without so many consequences.

Last week in the day-unit, a nurse had started asking her questions. Too many questions. She'd sat between her father and the boy, spinning out of control, unable to talk. Her father answered for her. Finally the nurse had gone away. She'd held the boy's hand — after all, he'd come up from South Carolina to be with her for this event, but strangely, it was her father's hand she longed to hold. They had the same strong shape of hand and long, fine fingers. Made to play the piano. But she could not remember holding her father's hand, ever. It was hardly the moment to begin.

"Shall I play it for you?" David asks.

They change places. David's eyes are very bad. He gets them checked at the hospital frequently. He adjusts his thick, heavily framed, green glasses to read the music. She remembers the odd message he has on his answering machine in which his voice says, "Greetings, carbon-based bipeds!" and as he starts to play, she thinks that he is part angel. Then, all language and thought leave her and she is in the music, the way she likes best, as close to God as she will ever be.

When the piece is over, she knows what nocturnal activities the music is describing. David is wrong. It is not about sex. It is a lullaby, a window opening to heaven, a place she likes, a place she knows is the beginning and the end even for unwanted carbon-based bipeds that are no bigger than her thumb.

There is a long silence in the piano lesson. Tripod jumps off the windowsill and is purring, rubbing himself against David's legs. She would do the same if she were a cat, but she can't purr or think of adequate words. So she smiles at her teacher. It's enough.

David smiles back, passes her the music and reads her thoughts. "That's what I'm here for: to inspire you."

"Thank you," she tells him. The lesson is over. It is time to go. She has made up her mind. She has to tell him.

"I have to cancel my lessons. I'm leaving. I won't be here next week . . . or for a while. I'm quitting school, every-thing. I'm going to South Carolina." She feels she owes him more of an explanation. She fights her shyness to tell him, "I have to find out what key I'm in."

She can't look at him. She senses unasked questions, but he pauses, maybe kindly, and says, "The nocturne — do you know what key it ends in?"

She shakes her head.

"You'll figure it out. Call me when you're ready to study again. I'll be leaving the Conservatory at Christmas. Teaching privately. You've got my number."

She leaves the large, rambling, red brick building. There are windows open on the upper floors where the rooms get hot and stuffy. She hears bars of music floating out to her like random thoughts, bits of jumbled conversations. She wonders how far they could carry on a good breeze, if she could hear them all the way in South Carolina. It is such a long way from here, a different country really.

She lifts her head at the sound of a familiar melody — heh! — the last bars of the nocturne. Is it possible? The music is no longer in a sad, minor key; it sounds sweet, like happiness. And suddenly she knows what key the piece ends in. She opens the manuscript to double-check, and is pleased. She's right. The C-sharp minor nocturne ends, amazingly, in C-sharp major.

Chopin just blows her away.

You Can Call Me Al

Brenda Hasiuk

The Friday night he rang the doorbell it was hot out, maybe thirty degrees, even though school had already started for the year. They weren't expecting anybody, and in Trish's experience anyway, when you're not expecting someone, nobody comes, except maybe fundraisers going door to door. The three of them were at the kitchen table eating barbecued chicken. Her mom was squinting at how much butter her dad was putting on his potato, and her dad was explaining what life was like before air conditioning, when the doorbell interrupted him mid-sentence. For a moment, they all just looked at each other like they'd never heard such a sound in their lives. And then her dad sighed and wiped his fingers and his mouth in the slow, careful way he did a lot of things. And as usual, her mom lost patience and began noisily sliding her chair to get the door herself. But it was Trish who, for some reason, actually said, "I got it."

So it was fifteen-year-old Trish who found Alexi standing there in the thick heat of a late Winnipeg summer. Later, this moment would sometimes fly into her head just before sleep and out again just as quick, as if it was almost too bizarre to think of as a real memory, as real life. There she was, expecting to see a kid selling chocolate-covered almonds or other junk her dad would have a good excuse to eat, and instead she finds a very sweaty young guy with a gold tooth, who holds out a ratty old suitcase like he's giving her a present and says: "I believe this is the residence of one Taras Dudek, and if this is the truth, then I believe you are my cousin."

And all Trish could do was stare stupidly. "Dad," she yelled. "I think it's for you."

Looking at it from the outside of course, it wasn't really that bizarre. Her dad's name was in fact Taras, a common name for Canadian-Ukrainian boys on account of the great Taras Schevchenko, whose tragic, old poems Trish knew by heart because she spent every Saturday morning of her childhood in a church basement learning what a suffering hero he was. Though Trish's parents were both born in Winnipeg, she knew all about how her Ukrainian ancestors had suffered under the Poles or the Romanians or the Russian communists for centuries on end. And the Dudeks did in fact keep in contact with several distant relatives there, including Trish's grandmother's two half-sisters. Every six months or so, Trish's family would go to her Baba Dudek's and together they'd pack coffee and detergent and other boring things, along with some crisp twenty dollar bills, into a large box addressed to the capital city of Kiev. The last time they'd done it, her Baba had pointed at Trish like a gypsy sending out a warning, and said something like:

"You be glad I came here, so you can be a proud Ukrainian. Over there, they still don't have nothing. The communists are gone but now there is nothing but criminals. Honest people have to live eleven people, in-laws and all, in four rooms. What do you think of that, you an only child in that big house? Eh?"

Like usual, this left Trish slightly unsettled. When she listened to her Baba, part of her always felt like she should try to figure out what the heck her Baba was talking about, because somewhere in the complaining and lecturing and gossip, there was something that was somehow important. But the other part of her, the bigger part, felt like the only way she could stand to be with her Baba, or even love her, was if she just let it all go in one ear and out the other.

There was no ignoring, however, the strange, sweaty guy at the door. There he was, one of her Baba's half-sisters' granddaughter's cousins, stopping in for a visit on his way to see a business associate in Chicago.

"I, Alexi, am also a business man," he said, now standing and sweating in the Dudek's front hall. By this time, Trish was holding his suitcase by a handle that was barely attached. She still couldn't stop staring like an idiot, though. And her dad wasn't much better, just rocking back and forth on his heels like he always did when he was trying to make small talk at weddings or funerals.

Trish decided that Alexi didn't look any older than her real cousin, Darryl, who was twenty-two. And that his clothes were brand new — bright, white cross-trainers, dark blue jeans, and a Calvin Klein T-shirt that you could tell had never been washed because the sleeves still showed sharp creases in the cotton.

"So sorry, Alexi," her mom said, reappearing from the kitchen with a tea towel. "Chicken can be so messy." She spoke in Ukrainian with her ultra-friendly and polite voice. "So tell us, Alexi, what business are you in?"

Alexi flashed his gold tooth. "I am a business man, who is a family man as well," he replied in English. Everything about his face was round and soft, except for the sharp, almost eerie blue eyes that seemed to be soaking up not just the front hallway, but the whole living room and family room and kitchen. When he spoke, Trish could not help noticing that his breath smelled bad.

"This is why I thought why not come and take time to see the family in the Winnipeg."

This finally seemed to jolt her dad into action. "Well, come in, come in," he said.

"If we'd known you were coming," her mom added, "we'd have picked you up at the airport." Then she grabbed the suitcase from Trish and the handle ripped right off. When it went "thump" at their feet, her mom stared at it like she had no idea how they were ever going to get the thing into the house now. Trish knew she was probably distracted, trying to remember when the sheets on the spare bed were changed last — even though Alexi didn't look like the type to care.

"That is broken," he said, sitting in her dad's recliner and grinning. "No worries. And please, I prefer English, not Ukrainian, so English please. My friends, they call me Al. Like Paul Simon. You can call me Al. You know?"

Trish watched for her parents' reaction. Nothing in her experience had prepared her for someone from Ukraine who knew a song by Paul Simon and didn't want to speak his own language. Her dad gave Alexi what she had come

21

to recognize as his principal-face. Since she'd been about twelve, she'd noticed his mouth took on a special shape before talking seriously with one of his students. "I am your friend," it said, "and I am your superior."

Her mom was already going back to the kitchen.

"Paul Simon. Yes, of course," she said over her shoulder, still in Ukrainian. "But let me get you something, Alexi. When was the last time you ate?"

He shrugged, and shouted in English. "Please, no trouble."

Trish's dad sank down into the couch. "Ukrainian is fine, you know. We're all comfortable with it." His mouth eased into his proud-father grin. "It's Patricia's second language but her grammar is better than my mother's."

Alexi spun around to Trish and waved her in, as if it was his house instead of hers. "Patrooosia, eh?" he said, pronouncing her name in Ukrainian. He stretched the middle syllable like an owl hooting in the night. "So my little cousin is Patrooosia, the most beautiful Ukrainian name. But it's Russian or English for me."

That's when he pulled out a package of cigarettes and waved it at her dad. "When I was a little one, it was Russian in school, and now English is the words of business." He shrugged and put a cigarette to his lips. "Nothing but English."

Her mom came in carrying iced tea and cookies. She stared at the unlit cigarette like Alexi had just grown a second nose. But her voice was all politeness.

In Ukrainian, she said: "How long are you planning to be in Winnipeg?"

"Uuh, few months," Alexi answered in English, then laughed until the cigarette fell from his lips. "No, no, I mean, few weeks, maybe." Holding up his hands at the tray, he spluttered, "Please, I please you, none for me. If I speak truthfully, I would like right now more than anything to have this smoke and then bed. My time, it is all off, and I feel so sleepy my English is not so good."

So the evening ended with Alexi smoking in their backyard while Trish's mom changed the spare bed sheets.

🍂 🍂 🍂

In her own bed that night, Trish couldn't stop thinking about things, like how someone who looked so hot could turn down iced tea. Or what Alexi must have thought when he stood smoking by their pool and the rock garden and the cedar gazebo that Baba Dudek called "that fancy, screened shack." Or why, when her parents whispered about how wonderful it was that Alexi had miraculously raised enough money to escape the hardship and corruption of Ukraine, and that he seemed like a nice boy with ambition, it felt like they were trying to convince themselves that this was true.

Gradually, though, these thoughts just became words running through her head, like "bad, bad breath," and "blue, blue eyes," and the next thing she knew, it was Saturday morning and she was gasping for air.

Trish was not used to waking up like this, because her dreams were almost always boring or dumb. When she tried to remember them, they were usually something like her science teacher standing by their pool, telling her she'd missed a mid-term, and then blowing his nose exactly like her Aunt Syl. This time, though, she could not catch her breath, so she lay back on her damp pillow and tried hard to bring the dream back.

She'd been sitting by the pool with her friend Tonya, whose father was their Orthodox priest, and who competed with Trish, in a friendly way, for who could get the best marks, or pour the most tea at the supremely boring Easter luncheon. In the dream, she was mad at Trish for some reason and said in Ukrainian, "No wonder they always called you Sucky Trishy," which was what Dale Golding called her in Grade 2 just to be dumb. Then Alexi walked up and offered Trish a cigarette. Tonya said, "your parents are going to like kill you," and disappeared and then Trish and Alexi were dangling their feet in the water and she was smoking like she'd been doing it her whole life. "This is really bad for you," she said. Alexi just laughed and said, "Many, many things are bad for you, Patrooosia." Then she started coughing and spluttering and that was it.

Fully awake now, Trish realized she'd been hearing the shower running for a long time.

There was a knock on her door. "Ten-thirty, up and at 'em," her dad said. "If Alexi ever gets out of the shower, he wants to see Wal-Mart and then we're having lunch at Baba's."

All Trish wanted was to roll over and sleep some more. But she knew her mom wouldn't even knock. No matter how many times Trish asked her not to, her mom would come right in her room and open the blinds.

So Trish rolled out and got dressed.

❧ ❧ ❧

They were all ready and waiting in the van when Alexi came through the back gate, not quite finished his cigarette. His hair was still wet and slicked back like a mobster in the movies. Trish didn't think it suited his round face. He was wearing the same clothes, and already sweating a little.

"Good morning to you," he said, climbing in beside her. "In Ukraine, you know, Patrooosia, where I come from, they would make cars like out of tin, so when you are hit, squash, you're dead." He flashed his gold tooth like he thought this was funny. "In Chicago, I will buy a Jeep with a roof that opens."

In the rear-view mirror, Trish could see her dad's principal-face. "A Jeep, eh? I hope your friend in Chicago is doing really well."

Alexi just shrugged and smiled at Trish like they were sharing a joke.

At Wal-Mart, though, there was no smiling. It was like none of them even existed. Alexi just kept picking up stuff and putting it down with a very serious look. In the end, though, all he bought was some caramel corn in a giant tin with race horses on it, and a large bag of white sweat socks. And when her dad tried to pay, as a "welcome to Canada" gift, Alexi waved him away. "I got it covered," he kept saying. "I got it covered."

For most of the way to Baba Dudek's, Alexi and her dad babbled on about different kinds of cars. But when they started to get to the other end of town, where the houses were old, or abandoned or even boarded up, Alexi got quieter. Trish could feel his blue eyes soaking things up. As they approached the corner of her Baba's street, she noticed something was different.

"The dry cleaning place burnt," she said.

Her dad nodded and stared straight ahead. "They should clean that up. It's been months."

As they pulled up to Baba Dudek's house, Alexi leaned forward. He was close enough to whisper in her dad's ear. "Here, where your mother lives," he said, "it is poor conditions."

There was a strange silence, then, until they all started unbuckling and getting out of the van. Her dad slammed the door and looked at Alexi with a face that Trish didn't recognize. His cheeks were red and stretched. "It's been going downhill for twenty years, but she won't move."

Alexi crinkled his nose, like he didn't quite understand, or smelled something bad.

"She can be a stubborn woman," her mom added.

Suddenly, everybody seemed in a bad mood. Except for Baba Dudek, who was now coming down the front walk, shuffling pretty fast for an old woman who weighed over two hundred pounds.

"Come in, come in," she said in Ukrainian, grabbing Alexi's arm like she was afraid he'd run away. When he handed her the giant tin of caramel corn, she acted like it was the best present she'd ever had, better than the TV or microwave or other big things we'd usually get her for Christmas.

She led them to her tiny backyard and practically pushed Alexi into an old lawn chair. "Sit, sit," she said. Most of her Baba's yard was a vegetable garden, scattered with plastic pails. Trish and her parents sat on the rotting wooden storage bench that Trish's Mom called "that old coffin of hers."

Baba Dudek stood right over poor Alexi, breathing hard from the excitement. "I was the oldest sister," she said. "And you are the first one to come see me. At least that has changed." Her fat body shaded Alexi's face, so Trish could not read his expression. "Is it as bad there as they say? When I left, many, many years ago, people were poor, but honest. The fields were more beautiful than anything in the world. Now they say everything is ruined."

Alexi shrugged. "Your relatives are well," he said, in Ukrainian, "and they send you good wishes."

Her Baba nodded and licked her lips. Her eyes were watery and blank. When she turned to Trish and her parents, it was like she didn't even see them. "And you've already met my son and his family," she said, still staring into space. "Taras is a principal and Evelyn a teacher. Of course, you have already seen their house."

Alexi put a cigarette in his mouth and said, "It's a nice house."

Her Baba licked her lips again, and ran her hand over Alexi's head. "But let me look at you," she said. "You're a nice-looking boy. Still have your hair. How old were you when the radiation exploded all over? Heh? Four? Five maybe?"

It took Trish a moment to remember what her Baba was talking about — the nuclear accident at Chernobyl the year Trish was born.

Alexi lit his cigarette and grinned for the first time since the van. "That was a game for us," he said, still in Ukrainian. "We would play radiation monster. You know, after Chernobyl we had Geiger counters to test for radiation levels, so those were our magic swords . . . " He trailed off then, his blue eyes focused somewhere next door. "Real Indians!" he yelled in English.

Everyone turned to see Baba Dudek's neighbour, Irene, and her family, piling into their car. All of the Traverses, young and old, were dressed in traditional Aboriginal costumes, complete with headdresses.

Trish lifted her arm to wave, but immediately felt stupid because she barely recognized any of them now. When she was small, sometimes she played with the Traverse kids who were around her age — usually tag, or statues, or just goofing around — while her mom peered from behind the curtains in the front window. They were always there when they drove up to Baba Dudek's and there when they left, as if they played outside forever and never even went in to drink or sleep. Their clothes usually smelled stinky and sweet at the same time, and sometimes they did crazy things, like eat a bug just to see what it tasted like. Elmer, the oldest, had jumped off a roof for fun and broken his back.

Baba Dudek made a spitting noise. "They're going to a pow wow." Then she turned to Alexi. "The Indians, they like to dance but not to work."

Trish tried to ignore it, hoping Alexi wouldn't understand. But her mom threw her head back. "Mother, you know that's not true."

Baba Dudek pointed at her like the crazy gypsy. "Irene is my friend. I can say what I want."

Alexi didn't seem to hear any of it. He was completely cheered up now, jumping up and down to get a better look. "Like the movies. This is why you come to Canada, no? To see the real Indians! Do you see the feathers? Real feathers!"

And no matter how hard Trish tried over lunch, and all the way home, to convince Alexi that the Traverses did not normally dress like that, that it was just a special occasion, that they were just normal people, he would only smile and shake his head. "OK, OK," he finally said, flashing his gold tooth and winking as if to humour her. "Maybe this is so. But, Patrooosia, I saw them for myself. They were the real Indians. They look like in the movies. For real."

When they got home, Trish felt so tired all she wanted was to go to her room, and maybe talk to Tonya on the phone. After Alexi had kept asking if there were "discos, for the dancing, you know?" her dad had finally agreed to drop him off downtown, with instructions to call when he was ready to come home.

For some reason, when Trish talked to Tonya, she didn't mention Alexi at all. They just talked about regular, everyday things that had nothing to do with Indians or Ukrainians.

🍂 🍂 🍂

When Trish came down to breakfast the next morning, her mom and dad were in a state.

Alexi hadn't called.

And they didn't hear from him until the police brought him home in the middle of the afternoon.

He had tried to shoplift nine CDs from the Wal-Mart. Trish's dad talked quietly with the young female police officer in the kitchen while Alexi stood in the front hall. His white Calvin Klein T-shirt was dirty now with what looked like mustard, and his blue eyes seemed completely absorbed by his shoes. After fifteen minutes, the police officer left. She brushed passed Alexi and held up a finger. "You get one break here. So stay out of trouble."

Then her dad looked at him with the same strange face when they'd pulled up to Baba Dudek's, his cheeks red and strained. "I'm sorry, Alexi. Trish is fifteen. We can't have the police here. You'll have to leave."

Alexi didn't say anything, just went straight to the spare bedroom to get his broken suitcase.

Before he left, though, he stopped in Trish's room to say goodbye.

"I'm off to Chicago to see my businessman." Trish looked up from her magazine. It was just the same as when she'd first seen him — all she could do was nod like an idiot.

Alexi stood there, his suitcase at his feet, like he was hoping she'd start talking and he wouldn't have to leave. Then he reached for the portable CD player on her desk. He turned it over like he was inspecting it for defects.

"This is yours, yes?" She nodded some more.

Then he fixed his sharp, blue eyes on her like he was going to share some profound secret. "You know, when I was small boy, nobody in my country could play the CDs. The stores, they were empty. Now, the shelves are full, but you must be a thief to buy. There is no money. You see?"

Trish didn't know what was the matter with her, but all she could do was nod.

Part of her couldn't help thinking Alexi wanted her to give him the CD player, as a "farewell from Canada" present or something. And she felt like he was trying to make her feel sorry for him, to kind of manipulate her.

Because maybe he was a liar, maybe there was no busi-nessman from Chicago at all.

And another part of her suddenly hated her parents, madly and passionately, more than she'd ever hated the stupid things Baba Dudek said. There they were, the big, proud Ukrainian-Canadians, actually kind of relieved that he was leaving their nice, clean spare room.

They took things for granted. They took her for granted. Like how could her Mom barge into her room in the morning like she was five years old. And why did they always assume she would just come along with them. What if she'd had plans yesterday? She hadn't really, but what if she had?

Trish just kept nodding.

"It was pleasure to meet you, Patrooosia," Alexi said, carefully placing the CD player back on the desk.

It took every ounce of energy for Trish to find her voice. For some reason she could not name, she felt ashamed.

"You too, Al," she said.

And then he flashed her his gold tooth and was gone.

ʒ⋆ ʒ⋆ ʒ⋆

That night, she woke up from a dream around four. She was crying a little, but felt very calm, her breathing slow and even. There, in the dark, it was like there was some-thing only her sleepy brain could see, could somehow understand, but it was too late, because Alexi was never coming back.

In the dream, it had been raining CDs, and she and Alexi were running to escape them. The next thing she knew, they were sitting on her Baba's rotting old coffin. They were both soaking wet and then his head was in Trish's lap and she was stroking his slicked-back hair. Very quietly, she whispered a song that she did not recognize, like she was a mother whispering a lullaby even though she was fifteen-and-a-half and he was maybe twenty-two. Somewhere in the background, Baba Dudek was watching them and crying softly. Never in her life had Trish seen her Baba cry. It made her look so old, but like a little girl, too. On and on Trish whispered, until Alexi closed his eyes and smiled like when he saw his real Indians.

As she lay there in the dark wondering about the strangeness of it all, she turned to check the time on her clock radio. Tonya's voice rang in her ears: "When you don't get enough sleep, Trish, you get those little grey circles under your eyes." But this made her feel oddly ashamed again, this trivial thought about how she might look in the morning, so she closed her eyes and let the strangeness wash over her.

She played the dream over and over in her mind, whispering the lullaby, comforting Alexi and her Baba, until she fell back to sleep.

The Way Skin Grows

Treena Kortje

At Chloe Finch's place, if you don't take off your shoes at the back door you'll always be one of "those" kids according to her mother, Mrs. Finch. This is not a good thing. Especially for a guy like me. Maybe if I'd been wearing sandals that day things would have turned out different. You know, shoes that slide off and on real easy, not like the army boots I was wearing, the ones that go up to my shins and take fifteen minutes to unlace. Then again, Mrs. Finch would have considered me one of "those" kids no matter what was on my feet. And that day, it just happened to be my boots.

I'd only been to Chloe's place once and it wasn't for a social visit. She was my partner in art class and invited me over so we could discuss our project. Frankly, I don't know what the teacher was thinking when he paired us up together. Even though she lived just around the corner,

Chloe Finch came from the exact opposite end of the universe.

We lived in Prairie Heights, a pretentious middle-class neighbourhood where everybody owned a mammoth house with a triple-car garage and a swimming pool. Me included. Only we didn't actually own our house — it was given to us. Two years ago my Grandma decided to move to a trailer park in Arizona. "What do I need all this space for?" she had asked, and so Dad and I moved in. Truth is, we didn't need all that space either. Three of the bedrooms are still empty, and in the two years we've been there I've never even seen what the pool looks like beneath the tarp. Too much work, Dad says, too much money to keep it up. He'll never admit it, but I know the only reason Dad agreed to take the place was because of the garage. I know, because he parks his pickup on the street and uses the garage for his sign-making business. It's heated, so he can work in there all year round and save a whack of money renting warehouse space. I understand his logic, but I'd still give anything to be back in our old place. Even if that meant it reminded me so much of Mom.

Chloe Finch was a perfect example of the things I hate most in this world. Not only was she disgustingly rich, she was one of those kids who had three middle names and insisted on writing them all down when she signed her name. She came from the kind of family where she called her mom "Mother" and her dad "Father" and everybody else called them Mr. and Mrs. no matter how well you knew them. In other words, they were snobs. High-class, uppity, designer brand-name wearing, glossy-teethed, expensive-perfumed-smelling snobs who clucked their tongues at black army boots and hung their artwork on the walls the way you were supposed to.

The day I went to Chloe's house, the first thing she did was show me her family's private art collection. I don't know if she was just bragging or if she wanted me to feel fortunate for having her as an art partner. All I know is the Finch "gallery" turned out to be nothing but a big room that was once just two bedrooms with the separating wall knocked out — I could tell by the off-coloured strip of stucco on the ceiling and the closets at either end of the room. The gallery was pretty much empty except for two wooden chairs in the middle of the room — both sitting side-by-side and facing opposite directions — and with a bunch of paintings on the walls. Hanging right there at eye level where they were supposed to be, each with an individual light screwed into the wall above it. I couldn't see an extension cord anywhere.

The first thing that caught my eye when I walked into the gallery was a five-foot-wide painting of an artichoke. I could hardly believe someone took the time to use such an enormous space to paint such a simple thing. No shadowing. No layers. No colour except for that one shade of green. A one-dimensional artichoke. It reminded me of something you'd find in a kid's colouring book under the letter "A". I walked right up to it and Chloe followed.

"So, what do you think?" Chloe asked after a few seconds.

I looked back at her and she was smiling, eagerly waiting for my reply. Her teeth were really shiny and wet, like she had gargled with Vaseline or something. But of course I didn't tell her. Not about her sparkling teeth or that it was really a Doors poster I was thinking about — the one hanging in the living room of Grandma's house — or how Dad sprained his ankle when he fell off the couch trying to push the thumbtacks in.

"It's nice," is what I ended up saying about the artichoke. "Yeah, it's pretty nice. In fact, when I think about it, it's a perfectly good example of a waste of space."

I looked back immediately to see Chloe's reaction, and saw the smile instantly drop from her face. She glared at me and clucked her tongue. The sound was familiar. It was the same sound her mother made when she first saw my boots on her white ceramic floor.

Chloe spun around and walked out of the gallery. I followed her down the hall and into another big room where all the walls were covered with books and the furniture was extra large with lots of cushions.

"Nice rumpus room," I said, looking around.

"It's a study," Chloe said dryly, and sat down on the end of an overstuffed couch. I sat down too, beside her, but on the opposite end. Right on cue, Mrs. Finch swooped into the room with a tray of munchies: miniature dried toasts, yellow cheese, grapes, and green non-alcoholic wine coolers that tasted like mouthwash.

"Here you go, sweetie," Mrs. Finch cooed. "You kids have fun, okay?"

It made me itch.

Chloe reached down into the backpack she had brought with her and began pulling her school supplies out onto her lap. When she was finished she looked up at me and said, "So, I don't suppose you have any ideas, do you?"

That's when I remembered I had forgotten my notes. I reached over to the tray of food on the table and grabbed a miniature toast. "Sure," I said, and slid the toast between my teeth. I looked at her shiny teeth and smiled, "I've got lots of ideas."

"You forgot your notes, didn't you," she said, and started flipping through the binder on her lap. "Why should I be surprised."

"Hey," I said, sitting up straight on the couch. "I'm not a moron, you know. I remember the drift of it. Besides, it's pretty basic. Something about being environmentally friendly and showing the world how screwed up we really are."

"Not quite," Chloe said sarcastically, and snapped a piece of paper out of her binder. "Art Class, 30A," she read. "Working with your partner, create an original piece of artwork using the following guidelines. One: All materials must be recycled and/or recyclable. Two: Your project should communicate a message that depicts the social conscience of your generation."

"What a load of crap," I said, and popped a clump of grapes onto my tongue.

"Can you just cooperate please?" Chloe hissed.

"Well, it is!" I laughed, chewing on the grapes. "We're supposed to create an original piece of work, right? But then they give us all these stupid rules." I tossed the empty grape stem onto the table, but missed and it landed on the floor. "It's not how art works," I said.

"Yeah, and like you knows how art works," Chloe scoffed.

I'm not a violent person. But the way she looked me up and down, mocking me and clucking her vaseline-coated tongue, I could have drifted her upside the head. Hard, too, and it surprised me because I've never hit anyone in my entire life, let alone a girl.

"What," I said, raising my voice, "you think you need to have an art gallery in your house to appreciate art?"

"It helps," she chirped, and reached over to pick up my grape stem from the floor.

"What, that artichoke thing?" I laughed loudly. "You think that's art? Give me a break."

"It *is* art," Chloe glared at me. "And a fine piece of work, too. My father paid over six thousand dollars for it. But I guess I shouldn't have expected you to recognize quality."

And that's when I knew smacking her wouldn't have solved a thing and that I had no choice but just to show her. Looking back, I realize what a moron I was for even trusting her. Especially when I hadn't shown the painting to anyone before. Not even Dad.

❧ ❧ ❧

You don't have to be a genius to know that real life breakups are never like you see them on TV, not at my house anyway. At my house, nobody cried or moaned or got down on their knees and begged for a second chance. At my house, I came home for lunch one day and had a grilled cheese sandwich and a mother. The next day I came home for lunch and didn't have either one. It was that simple.

Things got pretty weird after Mom left, but they got even weirder after all her things disappeared — her clothes, knick-knacks, her favourite raspberry soaps — and I know for a fact it wasn't her who took them. I know, because one day I took a bag of trash out to the alley and found a big pile of plastic bags next to the bin. At first I wondered who the idiot was who left them there like that, but it didn't take long to figure it out. The first bag I opened was full of clothes, and when I shoved in my hand I pulled out a woman's summer blouse: white with short, billowy sleeves and a big triangular collar. I recognized it immediately. Across the front were tiny intricate flowers — lilies and tulips and roses — all in bright colours and entwined around a long leafy stem.

She brought it home from Mexico the time Dad took her on a holiday for reasons he never admitted to, but reasons I grew to understand. I remember how she showed it to me when she got home, how she traced all the petals with her index finger and said, "Look at this. Can you believe someone actually took the time to do this with their own two hands?" I was eleven then. Young and stupid enough to believe everything was going to be okay.

The closest Dad ever came to mentioning Mom was thirty-eight days after she left. I know, because I counted back on the calendar after it happened. We were sitting at the kitchen table eating supper. That night he'd cooked for a change — hamburger helper, a cucumber salad, and a store-bought apple pie for dessert.

"Hey, good supper," I said, but he didn't answer. A few minutes later he set down his fork with a crash and said, "Did you know the top layer of a person's skin sheds and re-grows about every thirty-eight days?"

I had no idea what he was talking about.

"Oh, yeah?" I said, "Where'd you hear that?"

"I don't know. I must have read it somewhere. Interesting fact though, isn't it."

"Not really," I replied. "It's pretty disgusting if you think about it. I mean, that's a lot of dead skin. Where do you think it all goes after it falls off? Onto the floor? In our beds? In our clothes? In between the cracks of the furniture? Gross. Maybe we should vacuum more —"

"It's just a simple fact," Dad said. He was irritated. "Just forget I even told you, okay?" It wasn't until after I'd counted back thirty-eight days on the calendar I realized what he was talking about. That what he was really saying was that technically we were rid of Mom for good. Any parts of us she'd ever touched would have fallen off by now, been vacuumed up or washed down the drain. The outside parts, anyway. I'm pretty sure the inside parts never shed away.

☙ ☙ ☙

That day at Chloe's house, I knew the only way to prove a guy like me knew anything about art was just to show her, so I convinced her to catch the bus with me downtown. Chloe didn't own a bus pass, and by the way she wedged her purse between her legs and gripped onto the strap, I don't think she'd even been on a bus before. I dug into my pocket for change and came out five cents short for her fare. The bus driver didn't notice.

We didn't talk on the ride downtown. I sprawled out on the bench across the aisle from her and watched her from the corner of my eye. If I looked hard enough, she really wasn't that bad looking, especially when I imagined what she really looked like beneath all the pink sparkles and glossy stuff. Dark hair with lots of long curls, high cheekbones, full lips. Chloe Elizabeth Desirae Lynn Finch. Her name was a mouthful, that's for sure.

I rang the bell and got off the bus on 22nd Street. Chloe followed and kept a safe pace a few steps behind. I knew she was embarrassed to be walking next to a guy in combat gear and big army boots. I was the farthest thing from being her type at all. But I didn't want to think about that. I just wanted to get where we were going.

We reached Bess Park along the river, and I took the path that led down to the water. Chloe got a little nervous. "I don't think we should go down there," she said. "Isn't that where all the freaks hang out?"

"Yeah, I guess it is," I said.

"Well, I'm not a freak," she said defensively, "and I'm not going down there."

"Hey Chloe," I said, and kept walking, "news flash: to some people you are definitely a freak."

I continued along the path until it got shady because of all the wild caragana bushes, closer to the path under the traffic bridge. I could hear Chloe's footsteps behind me.

"You going to show me where you buried your last body?" she chirped.

I didn't answer.

"Well, are you?" she said again.

"Don't be a bitch," I said, and picked up my pace.

"I'm not allowed down here, you know."

"Don't worry," I promised, "I won't tell."

"You better not," she threatened, and I laughed out loud. As if I'd even think of calling up her folks and ratting her out. God, that's all I'd need.

"Okay, we're almost there," I said. I was getting excited to see it. "Close your eyes and I'll lead you."

"I don't think so," she said firmly and instantly stopped walking.

"Oh God Chloe," I moaned, and turned around to look at her. "I'm not going to do anything to you. I just want it to be a surprise. Just close your eyes and stop being so paranoid."

She obviously believed me because she closed her eyes and didn't resist when I took her shoulders and started guiding her. As I carefully led her beneath the bridge to where the painting was, it occurred to me how stupid she was. I mean, what if I really was a freak?

"Okay," I said when I had her in the perfect spot. "Open your eyes."

Chloe opened her eyes. She looked up at the painting on the side of the bridge and didn't say a word.

"Well?" I said. "Do you like it?"

"Who did this?" she asked.

"What do you mean, 'who did this?' I did this."

"You did this?"

"Yes, I did this. So what do think? Do you like it?"

"You did this all by yourself?"

"Yes Chloe, I did it all by myself. Me, the dude who knows nothing about art, remember? Do you like it or what?"

"Oh my God," was all she said, and then we stood there for what seemed like a long time. Just stood there and looked up at what I'd done.

Neither of us had any money for Chloe's bus fare home, so we decided to walk. She was going to call her mom but I talked her out of it. Being late for dinner was one thing. Being late for dinner because she was down at the river with me was another. I didn't mind, though. It gave us a chance to talk.

We left the downtown core and followed the path along the riverbank, up towards where we lived. Chloe kept herself three safe strides behind me.

"So where'd it come from?" she called up to me.

"The painting?"

"Yeah. Where'd you get the idea from?"

I didn't want to tell Chloe the whole story. In fact, I didn't want to tell anyone the story. Some things are just better left unsaid. Some things are just private. Besides, I hate people feeling sorry for me.

"Well?" Chloe pried. "What's the story? Every piece of artwork comes from some kind of inspiration. What's yours?"

"It's nothing," I said, staring straight ahead at the path.

"Oh, come on," she insisted. "You don't paint something like that for nothing."

"It is nothing," I said firmly. "Just a design on one of my mom's shirts, that's all. No biggy. I just liked the look of it."

"Must have been some special shirt," Chloe jeered. She didn't have a clue what she was talking about.

"What does your mom do, anyway?" she asked. She just didn't know when to shut up. "I mean, I know your dad makes signs. I see his truck driving up and down the street all the time. But what about your mom? I don't think I've ever seen her before."

"No, you haven't," I said dryly. "She's dead."

"Oh, God," Chloe stammered. I couldn't bear to look back at her. "Oh God, I'm sorry," she said, "I'm an idiot. Jesus. I didn't know."

"Don't worry about it," I said over my shoulder. I knew my voice sounded flip. "How were you supposed to know?"

It was quiet for awhile. Chloe picked up her pace so she was right at my side, and we kept walking beside each other like that, neither of us saying a word. I could sense her discomfort. I could almost feel it myself, and I figured she was beating the hell out of herself inside her head.

"Don't worry about it," I said again, looking over at her. "I mean it."

Chloe stared ahead at the pathway. A strand of her hair found it's way into her mouth and she was chewing on it nervously. "I feel stupid," she said. "I'm sorry. I didn't know."

She looked over at me then and I watched the corners of her mouth lift into an awkward smile. "It must have been tough," she said gently, blowing the wet strand of hair from her lips.

"Yeah," I agreed, managing to grin. "It was. It sucked big time. It still does."

Chloe nodded sympathetically, then reached over and put her hand on my shoulder. "It's a beautiful painting," she said, squeezing my shoulder firmly. Her hand was soft and small. "I didn't know your mother or anything, but I know she would've loved it."

Don't move your hand Chloe, don't move your hand, I silently begged. But of course she did.

❧ ❧ ❧

I should've known better than to underestimate what can happen in a matter of weeks. After our walk down by the river, Chloe was real sweet to me at school — talking to me in the halls, walked home with me a few times, even introduced me to one of her friends. But then the cops showed up and I got arrested and after that Chloe avoided me like the plague. It took her awhile to realize I wasn't going to slap the shit out of her, and somehow she mustered up enough courage to corner me at school so she could apologize. By that time it had been a couple weeks since I'd seen her up close, and I'd forgotten how sparkly and glossy she was. She wouldn't look me in the eye when she spoke, and her voice was really quiet and shaky when she said the only reason she took her mother down to the bridge was because she thought my painting was so beautiful she wanted her mother to see it for herself.

"Really," Chloe said desperately, "If I'd known she was going to call the cops on you, I would have never shown her. I mean it. You've got to believe me."

"Sure," I said, and looked over her shoulder, down into the crowded hall.

"Could you redo it?" she asked. "Maybe not on the bridge this time, but on a piece of paper, you know? It's an original, right? You've got the general pattern in your head. You've got the shirt. Couldn't you just do it over? I mean, how do you know it wouldn't turn out better the second time around?"

"Sure Chloe," I said coldly, and this time I managed to look right at her. "Good idea. I'll just redo it. Thanks for the suggestion. You're amazing."

Her eyes filled up with tears, and when one spilled over it took a stream of pink glitter with it as it rolled down her cheek. I actually felt sorry for her. Not because she looked pathetic with all that crap messed up all over her face. Not even because she didn't mean to get my painting sandblasted off the bridge or have me stuck with a hundred hours of community work to deal with. I felt sorry for her because she didn't know I'd thrown Mom's Mexico blouse away. That after I'd finished the painting I'd climbed the stairs onto the catwalk of the bridge, smelt the blouse one last time then flung it over the railing and watched until the white fabric floated down the river into the night.

"My mother doesn't know you," Chloe said. Pink, sparkly tears were running down her cheeks. "Not like I know you. She just thinks you're one of those kids, you know? She watches the news all the time and she's convinced all those whacko kids go around killing everybody because they don't come from a family like ours. She just worries about me. I know it's stupid and I'm sorry. But you can't really blame her, can you? She doesn't know you at all or understand anything about — "

"Chloe," I interrupted and bent down so my head was right in front of hers. "Neither do you."

I turned and walked away from her. Walked down the hall, out the doors and headed straight across the field for home. I was so angry, so incredibly pissed off my knees were shaking and I thought my heart was going to snap right out of my chest. And the worst part was all I could think about was Chloe's hand. How soft and small it was on my shoulder that day. How warm.

When I reached the corner of my street I stopped. Turn left: my house. Turn right: Finch house. I took a deep breath. Then another. Then pivoting in my black boots, I turned around and headed straight back towards the school, picking up my pace and stepping away from the part of myself that was afraid of what I was going to do.

Dammed Waters

Keith Inman

The fishing line sang out like a mad bee, following the sinker on a high arch toward the weed bed. The lead weight landed with a big wallop. Josh watched the rings expand outward. That cast had gone almost as far as his dad's used to go. He clicked the bail on the reel and set the rod against the guardrail just down from Bailey's Bridge. Only the top quarter of the fibreglass pole would bend if he caught a big one. His whole rig almost went in yesterday by not setting it up properly. He had to lunge after it at the water's edge, eventually hauling in a carp almost two feet long and fat like a tire. His two friends, Billy and Scott, said he could sell it down at the market for enough money to buy cigarettes, a girlie magazine or ice cream if the clerk gave them a hard time. They had no way of getting it there, of course. Scott ended up throwing a stone at the fish's head. The sharp flint missed, burying itself into the soft brown mud. Billy quickly ran to find a big rock to drop on it. The thing was gulping for air. Its eyes rolled back, as if looking for help. Josh picked it up by the tail, cradling its head, and set it down in the water. The big fish swam out of his hands real slow, heading straight for deep water. Billy came back struggling with a big pointed rock. "What's-a matter with you?" he said, dropping the boulder down the incline. It rolled into the water with a big splash before sinking under the muddy surface.

Light glinted on the top gold eye of his fishing rod, pointing into a blue sky. The sun was past noon. George was a couple hours late and the fish weren't biting today. Josh wondered if he should start walking. He only had one more slice of bread for bait. This was his fourth cast with the last one. Cheapest stuff in the store. Could it hold! You just pull out the centre (no crusts) and squish it onto the hook, like making a fist. Maybe it stayed in your stomach like that, he thought. Would it roll around for hours until you ate again?

He dug out the last sandwich from his knapsack, then had to fight to get the wrapping off. The bread was squished at one corner. Peanut butter and jam oozed against the plastic. A full day old and a bit stale. He crumpled the waste wrap into a ball and pushed it into his pants pocket. Whatever this bread was it sure took away the stomach pangs.

Billy and Scott would have been home a long time ago, and eaten a decent lunch with a tall cold glass of milk. They'd ridden their bikes up to the lake yesterday morning. Josh had been able to convince his big, bothersome brother George to drive him up with all the equipment, early Saturday afternoon. The boys were camping out for the weekend: doing some serious fishing, they'd said. However, heavy rains flooded the tent Saturday night. When morning arrived and they hadn't slept, Billy and Scott packed up their soggy sleeping bags and left.

Josh told his two departing friends that he'd wait by the bridge for George, and catch an even bigger carp. "Buy a gallon of ice cream," he said. He'd be all right. Home was a few kilometres away. This is where he fished all the time, riding his bike on sunny afternoons.

As the two boys walked their bikes through the early mist out to the road, Josh yelled that he'd thumb a ride if he felt like it. "Sure you will," echoed back. Then the boys said something to each other that Josh couldn't hear, as they disappeared into the evergreens.

He reeled the line in a foot or two, to give the bait some action. From the tip of the rod, he followed the thin, clear monofilament to where it disappeared into the lake. A few years ago, his dad had tied two cans to a string, handed Josh one, and walked over to the shed. They were about thirty feet apart and Josh could hear the voice in the can like a distant echo, or a seashore voice in a shell. It was neat for about three seconds, then it was "Get into computers Dad!" But his dad never did. He liked neat stuff, but it had to be easy or mechanical, like a lawnmower, or he'd get frustrated and angry. He didn't fish with Josh anymore either, which was all right. With Billy and Scott, that wouldn't be cool.

A car pulled through the crossroads and parked on the little strip of boulevard no more than twenty feet away. It was angled on the grass fancy like, out of the way of traffic. The passenger door on the old green car swung open. A chubby man sat sideways, smoking a cigarette, his feet up on the seat, an arm stretched along top. It made him look like he was relaxing in a cave. He held out a cigarette. "Catch any today? Looks good for catfish."

Josh turned back to carefully inspect his line. He wasn't supposed to talk to strangers. You can't pretend to be deaf, he thought, and tightened the line even more. He supposed this could be more like talk between fishermen. "Fishing for carp," he called over his shoulder.

"They're calling for a lot more rain this afternoon. That's why I packed it in. Only got a big old five-pound bass this morning." The man tried not to smile. "Got it across the canal."

Josh had heard stories like that. He wasn't allowed over there, although Billy had taken him a couple times. It was no big deal.

"You can see the rain comin' in. See! Over there. Need a ride?"

Josh glanced up and noticed dark grey clouds beyond the highway, and wondered what was holding George up. Maybe he'd forgotten or been called in to work. A ride now would save Josh a load of pestering from George, who's hitchhiked all over the place, even out past the tobacco farms. He's told Josh about huge square fields, kilometres long and wide, of just mustard plants, "Yellow as the stuff in the bottle."

This guy seemed okay, knew about fishing, and didn't look much taller than Josh, who could outrun him that's for sure.

The clouds to the west were building. A leading edge of grey started to divide the sky into sections, giving up space to the rain.

He reeled in. There were no takers today. Maybe next Saturday, he thought.

"Just toss your Hobo bag in the back seat there. Wanna smoke or a coke?"

"No thank you." He'd be home soon.

Josh told the man which roads to take and they drove off, exchanging pleasantries about weather, fishing, and sports. But not names. Even when Josh gave his, the man talked about the town, its hospitalities, and the new generating station. All the while, smiling, a wry kind of smile. George would say it'd fall off his face if he tilted sideways. Float like a feather to the ground. George had something to say about everybody.

The round man with the short pickle legs grabbed a clipboard from the dashboard and began looking at it. "I'm doin' some work up at the hydro dam. I'm one of the engineers. Got all the plans right here. S'pose ta be there today. If I feel like it. Not sure how to get there though. Like I said, I'm new in town. Know how to get there?"

Yes he did. But Josh had seen plans before. Last year his dad brought new house plans home from work. Ma had stopped that real quick as he and the two boys pored over the big sheets on the kitchen table. This fella's clipboard was only full of numbers. He seemed to be putting on a show, as George would say, "Trying to make a few toonies sound like a ten spot." Besides, with barrel shorts, twisted socks and scruffy runners, he looked more like a labourer, like George, who Dad always said, "blows all his money on cars, booze and acting tough," which he wasn't really. Except for pushing Josh around.

Josh thought this stranger was a bit of an oddball, kind of funny, not like a clown though. And some people just didn't get road directions easily. He remembered his dad one time, patiently going over a map with an old couple from out of town. Eventually all the turns along the red snaking roads were marked with circled Ls or Rs. Josh explained the road directions to the engineer, carefully and slowly, so the fellow would understand, but he said he'd never find it, kept turning in his seat, driving with one hand on the wheel, glancing up at the road now and again.

"I really need to get there. Are you sure you wouldn't mind going for the drive, maybe make a few casts? You should make time. Help a 'new neighbour' in town."

It was a bit far. Josh had to be back in time to tell George that he didn't need a ride. "No, I have to get home."

"How 'bout I give you some money. Ten bucks for being a nice kid. Here!"

"No, that's all right." Josh would take George's money, but not a new person in town.

Then the stranger offered to return the favour of directions by doing something to Josh. Astonished, Josh made his voice say no. The stranger asked if Josh would do it to him. Josh stammered no.

They drove on in near silence, the only sound, the murmuring engine as the roadside rushed by. If Josh jumped, he'd be all scraped up and bleeding in the ditch, probably with a sprained ankle. Unable to run, the man would catch him, or drive over him maybe.

They passed a hydro tower. The generating station was that way.

He looked at his hands expecting to see them shaking, but they weren't. They just stayed wherever he put them, although they seemed hard to move. He tapped the armrest alongside the door handle, and tried to look around like his mom did on the long drives up north to the cottage. She'd always start reading the road signs aloud.

There were no road signs here, just ditches, posts and barbed fences racing by.

The tall metal framework of the canal-bridge stood out across the far field.

"Don't go wandering off across the canal," his mom used to tell him. "There's undertows there by the dam." Lately though, she's been telling him to, "Always go with a friend," because she knows he's been there with Billy and Scott.

Billy would know what to do.

A small group of houses loomed up on the right. People were in the front yard of the larger one, shaking hands and hugging. A group of kids played off to the side. A small boy waved to him. Josh hesitated then waved. "You can drop me off here. This is fine. Billy just saw me, his dad — He'll give me a ride home."

The stranger tapped the steering wheel. "Yeah. I'll give you a ride home. Right after the dam."

Josh forced himself to stare at the side of the round face, "I live th'other side a Billy's field." His voice quavered a bit. "He'll wonder where I was goin' — in a green car. I'm late already."

The man stared at the road. Then pulled over. Josh could hear the soft shoulder of the road crushing under the tires. He reached for the door handle while they were still rolling.

"You did the right thing. I was just testing — you — you passed. Take care of yourself!" The last bit was said very loudly. But he didn't offer to back up to the house.

Josh grabbed the pack quickly from the back seat as the man waved a spent match in the air. The smoke distended out from his short pudgy fingers toward Josh. "Hey! Thanks for the directions. Be a good kid, eh."

Josh nodded and stepped back. The pack rolled to the ground.

He slammed the door.

The car tore into loose gravel. Josh ran to the tall grass searching for a good weapon. Tires screeched on pavement. He swept armfuls of weeds aside, until a round, weighted stone appeared. Jumping up, he whirled around, to find the car driving slowly away, as if nothing was wrong. Had the wheels just spun in the stone?

He stood poised like an archer, eyeing the back windshield, the rock turning over in his damp fingers. His ma's voice downloaded into his head (*It's wrong to throw stones*). Sweat broke over his brow. His hands fell limp at his side. Billy would have thrown it. Maybe. Josh remembered a few weeks ago, Billy over late one night with a black eye and bruising up his arms. His dad — drunk again. "When does something turn into a lie?" Billy asked him. He was sure then that he didn't know.

The target grew smaller.

In a flash of sun, the dark car turned a corner at the hydro lines and headed toward the canal. He watched it pass behind the trees of the side lane. Each opening taking it further away, until it was gone.

The stone dropped, clicking on the ground below him.

Why hadn't it sped away? Then the rock could've been hurled, smashing out the back windshield. Josh would've run, jumping the ditch, across the fields, cut through the Sand Hills and by Cecchini's pond. He would've been home late but that guy wouldn't't've caught him, didn't know which house Josh lived in. He never told him.

The knapsack sat at the roadside like a rumpled green lump. All his camping equipment was there, his fishing rod and sleeping bag, soaked from rain, rolled up and tied on top — his name and address on it. It would've slowed him, but he'd've grabbed it as he leapt over the ditch.

He kicked a big tuft of weeds along the ditch, shooting off a short volley of loose stones. The pack was heavy on his shoulders. It threw him off balance. A voice in his head said, *No swearing. You know better than that.* He grabbed a handful of stones, ran a couple steps and hurled them as hard as he could down the road. They scattered into the air, and fell on the soft tarmac like a sheet of rain.

High up, the sun was making its way down onto the farms on his right. A big shiny car pulled onto the road, and drove off in the other direction. People in the driveway waved and yelled "Good-bye!" and "See ya!" He turned away and headed up the road toward a tall stand of pines.

The ditch beside him was alive with clear running water, the bottom lined with small pebbles. Every so often, a small jumble of sticks held back the rushing water, some of it draining away into muddy turbulence. He could've never run away from the man and got far. The fields were swamped with last night's rain. There'd be no shortcuts. He was probably going to be late for dinner — Sunday dinner. All because of a free ride that had taken him farther away from home than he was this morning.

He rounded the corner of Merrit's farm toward Cecchini's, and home.

A cluster of wrens fluttered at each other in a tangle of bushes and wire fencing. The three bigger ones seemed to be mad and were picking on a smaller one. They chirped up quite a row. The little one broke free and swooped out of the hedge, staying low, flying down and across the lane.

Josh figured it would definitely be better if he made it on time for dinner. If not, he'd need a story — would he tell the truth? Would the truth sound like a lie? — A big lie. Would they believe him? He'd be attacked with questions that would ring in his head; answers would stick in his throat like dry toast.

The narrow straps of the pack dug into his shoulders. He shrugged it up, trying to remember the car. A green Chev? It smelled like toilet-bowl cleaner. Had a clipboard full of numbers. The front seat was faded and cracked where you sat. The man — not old, had no hard wrinkles like a granddad. Was more his father's age, only shorter, plumper. Had a round, chubby face with straight brown hair in a bowl cut. Had to stretch to reach the gas pedal and brake.

He wiped his sleeve across his eyes and shifted his pack to the other shoulder.

There was a damp spot on his cuff.

To the far right, across Cecchini's vineyard, the sun reached for the tops of the poplars that sectioned off the pears. He'd been caught the only time he ever stole them. His dad took away all computer rights for the rest of the year. That seemed like ages ago — a very long winter.

Shadows from the fence had crept out of the ditch toward him. He turned right where the old rusted fence was grown into a huge, gnarled tree stump, marking the crossroads for Lines Seven and Four.

A daunting line of dark grey passed by to the south; the rain had missed them. Now, the bright low sun shone the length of the whole street, forcing him to look down.

The toes of his shoes were splattered with small bits of tar from the road's soft edge.

He always made the towels dirty too, his mom said. She would fluster if he told the whole story. Dad'd be mad, asking if he got the licence plate number. 8QB or BO3? His big brother George would slap him on the shoulder, saying not to worry but he'd 'a nailed the guy right in the Nuts!, veered the car at a telephone pole and jumped out in a breath of time.

Turning the last corner, the house stood dark under the willow tree, the long strands hanging motionless. His mom would be on the couch watching the news. She would easily spot the worry, maybe mistake it for guilt. His father would toss the paper aside and stand up from his worn, layback chair, the form of his body still imprinted in the bulky stiffness. "Where the hell have you bin? Your mother's bin worried sick." His voice will shake the china.

Josh loved to sit in that chair and smell the pipe smoke settled into the fabric. It was always best when you flopped into it.

"Well young man!" The boom would drop, the story blurt out, except why he got into the car. He couldn't remember now. If he was asked that, he'd have to shrug his shoulders, and that always made his dad get louder.

Walking softly up the sidewalk, he heard the sound of dinner dishes rattling from the kitchen window. He stepped lightly, had the pack off now, hugged in front of him, working his way along the siding to the corner and around to the back of the house. George's car was pulled

up on the grass out back. Josh opened the screen door carefully, only to have the hinges call out.

He set the pack down in the corner of the landing on
top of some shoes. That couldn't be helped. His breath
seemed to betray him, coming fast and hard. He stole the
stairs one at a time, rounded the hall corner and headed
quietly up toward his room.

"Joshua! Come Here! Now!"

He stopped mid-step, as the voice blew by like a storm.

His eyes went dry, as if a wind was in them.

Then the tears welled, and the dam started to burst.

Dream

Erica Tesar

He will not come. I thought I'd get something to take the pain away. I wish they would take my thoughts away. I think it will be born tomorrow. My birthday present to me. No happy returns! God, take these pains away. The nurse doesn't like me. I am a slut, she is silently saying. Wise voices oft said, over and over, again and again, "What were you thinking? He is a man, dear. What would he see in you?" Puppy love makes babies. Please send $100.00 and SASE for recipe.

"I'll have it," says sister Maria.

"We'll have it," says parents who are not mine.

"I'll have it," says the father not-to-be. Those ice-blue staring eyes below the pale blonde hair.

I will never be the me I am today, ever. No more solos. Push, pant, breathe, hum. You are too young. I am too young. But if I didn't know, time I would not be too young. I am only too young because the doctors say so, the teachers say so, the parents say so, the priests say so. Yes, yes I am too young because I do not want it. I feel as if I'm screaming but nobody is looking at me so I suppose I am not.

Awful thoughts invade my day. These thoughts flash like adverts across my mind and like all adverts they recur too often. I would like to think I am dreaming but I know I am not.

When I was six and lovely — God that was not so long ago, I had big brown eyes and long, long eyelashes that curled at the end. Grown-ups used to talk about them. Now they are lost in a pudgy face. My hair wasn't long and it wasn't short, grown-ups did not talk about my hair. That was the year I got a doll for my birthday. I knew it was a doll before I opened the box. My mum wanted to cut the string but I opened it very slowly, all on my own. I lifted off the lid, very gently, and pushed back the paper and there it was, a doll. Uncle Fiorello had sent it all the way from Italy.

It had red lips, blue eyes and pink panties that came off, whooosh, just like that.

It had a dress that was prettier than my party dress.

My baby is a secret because we are Italian. My very best friend knows, my teacher knows, my doctor knows, my parents know, his Swedish parents know, the priest knows, I HAVE SINNED.

My mum said the doll was beautiful. My dad said, "Mama Mia!"

So I threw it in my buggy and took it for a walk. I walked over the bumps to my very best friend's house. She liked it a lot and her mum picked it up and gave it a kiss, so I left and pushed it to High Street.

I don't know if I will have a very best friend when I walk out of here. I won't be swimming at the lake, pitching for the team, sleeping over, if I keep it.

It sat up all the way and people kept stopping me all the time. People I didn't even know would smile, not at me but at it. They asked me where it came from. They asked me how old it was. They told me it was lovely. They told me I was lucky. I said nothing.

Sometimes, when I take my dog for a walk the same thing happens. I feel as though I am invisible. The nurse thinks I am crying for the pain, I am, but not that pain. Will its crying keep me awake at night? Will my music keep it awake at night?

I took it to the drug store, I remember that because I knew the lady and she let me go to their secret washroom. I took it with me and I noticed that one of its blue, blue eyes had just a bit of a squint. It had hardly any eyelashes. But when I undid the braids its hair touched its bum. And it had no freckles.

Why am I remembering all these tiny details? Pant, pant breathe. Freckles that multiply like tin coat hangers. People put hangers up themselves. Now, that is a sin. You can die, I could die tonight, it could die, but it won't.

The lady at the store bought me an ice cream because I told her it was my birthday. She loved the doll.

I took it outside and laid it flat on its back in the buggy.

Somehow it got chocolate ice cream all over its dress. When my mum saw what a mess it had made, she said she'd make it a new one. I said, it could have shorts like mine. Mum said nothing and nothing means, no.

I've had a lot of nothing lately. She made me a dress for the bump. She doesn't know, I know, but in her bedroom hidden in a box is a layette. Click, click, knit, knit, cluck, cluck. Pant, pant — no swearing.

My dad picked it up and said he would make it a bed. A whole bed to itself. Then, as if it was nothing, he sat it down on his chair. The cat couldn't sit in his chair. I couldn't sit in his chair. Mum couldn't sit in his chair. But it could. It watched me blow out the candles on my cake. Dad kept saying silly things to it.

He's like that with his parrot. And he'll be like that with — it, if I take it home. He doesn't know that I know, there's a wooden cradle in the basement, next to the wine vat. Will they give it all away like a package deal? Will they have a party without me tomorrow? Will it get cards for being born?

Dad wanted to call it Sophia. Mum wanted to call it Anna Maria.

I took it to the washroom. Washrooms hold more secrets and tears than any other room.

It had a tiny accident. It fell off the basin into the lavatory, head first. I saved its life by yanking its leg. What a mess!

Will it have all its parts? The picture says it will. The picture showed me what it is. That is the only secret I have, the only private part of me, somehow it helps this pain me knowing.

I pulled off its dress and scrubbed it clean.

I am frightened of this memory.

I cleaned it all over. It had no marks anywhere. I scrubbed its red, red lips. It didn't hurt.

Just like the doctor says and that is a lie. They do things to your body that I could never speak about, just to make you clean.

Its hair was such a mangled angled mess I had to cut it to get the knots out. I cut it not too short and not too long, just like mine.

They want me to cut my hair, my hair that I can sit on. They say when you have a baby your hair falls out. They say I will not have time to look after my hair. I say . . . no, that is not true, I say nothing, am too hurt, too angry to say anything. Can't they see how precious my long, long hair is to me? I will be an architect one day. Now I am building a new creation on such shallow ground. I am frightened I will be . . . I cannot say it.

Then I got my mum's brown stuff and I gave it freckles. It looked really lovely.

They say I glowed as I growled! I may have stretch marks where my skin has stretched to make a home for it. They never go away. Is that to remind me that I have sinned? My wounds for life for giving life. Do good girls get stretch marks?

I showed my doll to the mirror and she looked a lot like me. Then I wrapped her in my very own towel, I hugged her and loved her and I took Lucy doll to bed with me.

She is waiting for me in the Maternity Ward bed. Not this bed. This is the birthing bed. Will it like it? They sleep in clear plastic containers, like storage bins. Birth beds, death beds. God, help me to know what to do, I am so afraid. I have a name band on my wrist so they will remember who I am. They will give it one as soon as it is born. I have such vain thoughts. Will my belly be baggy and saggy? Will my breasts be normal — oh, the milk, I forgot about the milk. He is older, older and not afraid. He is a grown-up. I am a discard. One day he would give it a new mother. I would be shut out. Will anyone ever want me and it? Will they want to be a daddy to another man's child? If it has pale, blue eyes and hair so flaxen will my sister want to take it back to Italy? Push, push, breathe. Oh, God please, please take this pain away. I cannot see the doctor, she is beyond my knees.

"Nurse, don't go." There is a voice calling her. I hear voices that are stabbing into my pain.

"That is my child. I have rights."

"That is our grandchild. We have rights."

"I am its aunt."

"Would you like someone to be with you? No? Then, happy birthday. Hold my hand. Short breaths, pant, pant."

Happy birthday to me. So my parents made me the same day as I made it. Seventeen years and forty weeks ago. Good-bye, my not-so-sweet sixteen. 40 Sundays, 40 Mondays, 40 Tuesdays, push, 40 Wednesdays, push, push, 40 Thursdays, good good, 40 Fridays good girl, its — 40 Saturdays. Saturday's child. Don't let them take it away. Don't cut the cord, then no-one can take her away. I shall call her Ashling. Ashling, a dream. I cannot give a dream away, I would be lonely for my dream. And I will be lonely with it.

First Snow

Gillian M. Savage

The usual crew is hanging out in "the pit", the covered part of the bleachers behind the school. Tommy Bloom and his buddies are there smoking, along with Angeline, Becky and a pair of tough-looking girls from eleventh grade. The heels of my boots clop on the frosty blacktop and I pull my black vinyl jacket closer around me as I trot up to the fence, shivering. Leather would be warmer, but I can't afford it.

"Hurry up, Pauline," Ange calls as I reach the rectangular door cut in the wire fence. She's holding out a smouldering joint.

"Too early in the morning for it," I say. Ange's nickname for me is Polly Prude, a name she made up the night we managed to sneak into one of the two bars in our town. I got bored talking to drunken mill workers and left too early for Ange's taste.

She smiles, blowing smoke, then pulls back her frizzy blonde hair and stuffs it inside the sheepskin collar of her denim coat. "Makes the day go smoother. C'mon."

"Thanks, but I gotta stay alert or I'll flunk biology and they won't let me graduate next spring. They'll hold me back like Tommy." I dump my purse down on one of the benches and root for my pack of cigarettes. I light up and suck in, then cough and wheeze. Damn things are giving me asthma.

"You going to the ravine with us after school?" she asks.

The ravine is at the edge of town, a wooded area past the new recreation centre. Not many people go down there, especially at night. There are rumours of ghosts. Last February a girl from our school went missing. Her name was Jane. She was a grade younger than me, but I used to smoke with her in the first-floor girls' bathroom. The day she went missing, she was hanging out at the ravine with friends. She went to take a pee in the bushes and never came back. At first they thought she'd run away, but then the police found her purse.

I shrug, aware of Ange's eyes on me. "Dunno," I say. "It's getting dark earlier these days. Too cold. Feels like it's gonna snow."

She nods, her eyes glazing like something else is on her mind. Or the pot's taking hold. "Tommy likes you," she says.

I stare at her, blowing smoke upwards. "What happened to that red-haired girl?"

Ange takes a drag of her joint, squinting up her eyes, then flicks the nub away with a look of regret. "He dumped her last week."

"Hm," is all I can say. The buzzer sounds and it's time for class. We all walk back as a group, Ange beside me, and I notice Tommy shoots a few looks at me as he jokes with his buddies.

"You seen the new kid yet?" asks Ange.

I shake my head.

"We saw him crossing the field this morning, and Tommy called him a geek." She laughs.

I roll my eyes.

"Tommy's funny, don't you think?" demands Ange. "I wish it was me he liked."

We reach the door to the school and I throw aside my cigarette butt. I don't know why Tommy would prefer me to Ange. She's pretty, with a small pointy nose and big blue eyes, and she's skinnier than me although a bit flat-chested. Tommy must like big boobs. He's definitely the "bad boy" type, with thick dark hair and a bony face. I admit the thought of him liking me gives me a tight, excited feeling in my throat. I can't help picturing myself on the back of his motorbike with my arms around his waist.

I say goodbye to Ange and take a deep breath to prepare myself for Biology class. Today we're dissecting rats. I walk into the class and immediately spot the new kid. A thin boy with brown hair, tanned skin and big sad eyes like a cocker spaniel. He looks too young to be in this class. As soon as everyone sits down and gets quiet, Mr. Wood makes a big deal out of introducing him.

"This is Harry. He was born in Canada but he's been living in Brazil where his father worked as an engineer. Harry has never seen snow before, so I told him we'll be getting some very soon."

Mr. Wood laughs like he's made a big joke. Sure enough, I think, this kid will soon get more snow than he could ever want. After eight months' worth he'll wish he'd never heard of northern Ontario.

"Harry's in town because his father is upgrading the machinery at the mill," Mr. Wood explains. "Stand up and say hello, Harry."

The boy glances at the floor, stands up reluctantly and says, "Pleased to meet you."

His voice is formal and has a bit of a Spanish-sounding accent. A few people snicker, and Harry hunches over and sinks back down like he wishes he could burrow into the floor. He raises a hand to his chest, then pulls an asthma inhaler from his pocket and takes a puff. My lungs twinge in sympathy.

We get on with class and I nearly puke but finish the rat dissection. By the end of the day, I meet Ange at my locker and she reminds me about the ravine.

"Aw, no. Let's just go to the mall or something."

She shakes her head. "We went there yesterday. What's wrong with the ravine? It was fun last time."

I open my locker to avoid answering. Sure. It was fun to a point. Until Ange and Becky went off to the rec centre to use the can. Naturally the boys were too manly for that type of thing and went into the bushes to piss. So Tommy, drunk, suggested a contest. Until then I thought "pissing contest" was just an expression. I looked away while they did their thing. Tommy ended up losing, and he got so mad he started hassling the boy who'd won, saying it was easier to fire from a short gun. They started pushing and shoving. I said I wasn't staying to watch a fight, so Tommy called me a prudish bitch and the others laughed.

Then we heard the voices. We thought maybe it was some kids from our school, but it was dark by then and we couldn't figure out where they were. We walked around looking for them, but the voices didn't seem to get louder in any one place. It was creepy. Finally Ange and Becky came back and asked why we were all so quiet. The voices had faded by then but nobody felt like hanging around.

There's no way I'm going back to the ravine for more of that crap. By the time Ange and I leave school there's a half-foot of snow on the ground and more big white flakes drifting from the sky. Our breath makes clouds in the stinging air. I decide to go home and make hot chocolate, maybe talk on the phone.

So wouldn't you know I end up at the ravine anyway, freezing my ass off and my hair covered with melting snowflakes. As soon as we arrive, I know it's a mistake. Tommy and his handful of buddies are drunk on beer, as I can see from all the empties lying around. Ange and I are the only girls.

"Let's go," I say to Ange. "Too cold out here."

But someone gets a smouldering fire going under the high skirt of a pine tree, where there isn't much snow. Ange has a sampler bottle of whisky she shares with me, which helps warm us up. One of the boys, Bill, is talking about the last time we were here.

"I told my dad about those voices, and he said there's a legend about this place. Back when my grandpa was young, there was a ranch in this area, and lots of people went missing in the ravine during winter storms. You couldn't even use a compass down here because there's a magnetic field in the rocks that pulls the needle off, and it gets stronger when there's snow. The Indians said there's bad magic here. Anyway, everyone thought those missing ranchers froze to death, but nobody could find their bodies after the snow melted. And people travelling past on the road said they heard voices, or saw figures walking among the trees, especially in winter."

There is a long pause.

"Come to the da-a-ark side," growls Tommy in a Darth Vader voice, and we all laugh. Bill picks up his beer and chugs it down.

It's past dusk now, although it still seems bright because everything is blanketed in glowing white. The snow is coming down fast, but one of the guys points out a figure at the top of the ravine, near the rec centre. It gets closer, walking slowly down through the trees — a teenage boy, it looks like, but he hasn't seen us. He's acting strange, walking slowly in circles, holding up his mittened hands to the sky. As he turns toward us, I recognize his face.

"Hey, it's Harry," I say. "He's playing with the snow like a little kid."

"Who?" asks Ange. "Oh, the new kid." She follows my gaze. "He looks like a retard."

The boys laugh. Harry bends to pick up handfuls of the snow. He puts some in his mouth, then throws the rest out in a shower over himself.

"It's the first time he's seen snow," I explain.

Tommy stands up. "Well let's show him what it's good for." He turns and looks expectantly at the group.

"What?" says one of the other guys.

Tommy grins. "Wash his face for him."

"Aw, grow up, man. It's too cold for that crap."

But Bill stands. "Think we could get him?"

"Sure," Tommy drawls. "He's not even looking. C'mon, it'll be fun." He and two others start climbing the hill, staying close to the trees. The other guys look back and forth at one another, then follow, with Ange and me behind them.

"This is stupid," I pant as we jog to catch up, our shins plowing through the soft snow and our breath trailing out in streams of mist. Harry, up ahead, is still looking at the sky.

Harry turns and sees us through the veil of falling white flakes. He stands and stares, bewildered, like a raccoon in the headlights of a car, like he's not sure we're a threat. Finally he starts running.

I think at first they won't catch him. Bill is a sprinter on the track team, but he's also drunk. Then Harry, looking back over his shoulder, stumbles and crashes down. He gets up and starts to run again, but Bill catches up and grabs his collar.

The struggle is silent, like TV with the sound off, as Tommy and Bill push Harry to the ground and pull open the neck of his ski jacket. They're bigger so it's no contest. Then Tommy gets a handful of powdery white into the boy's tanned face, and Harry starts to howl. I can hear them laughing as they hold him down. I got face-washed myself as a kid, before I learned how to fit in. I remember the freezing pain of that innocent-looking snow, like a zillion pins stabbing into you.

We catch up. The other boys and Ange are all laughing as the three guys holding Harry shovel snow over him, in his face and down his shirt. His eyes bulge with panic. He sputters and coughs. I remember how it feels to be held down, the suffocation as the burning-cold snow constricts your throat, ice water dripping into your nose and mouth. Tommy straddles his chest, holding his arms, as Bill pulls off his toque and crushes snow into his hair. The third guy, whose name I don't know, shoves snow down the waistband of Harry's jeans. Bill is holding his arms now as Tommy dumps more snow on his face.

Harry is coughing and gasping as he tries to say something. I remember his asthma.

"Stop!" I yell, stepping forward. "He can't breathe! You're hurting him."

Nobody listens to me. It's like we're underwater or something. Everything's in slow motion and my arms and legs feel weighted. I'm so cold I've stopped shivering and my brain feels numb. The falling snowflakes are huge, like white feathers. It's hard to see clearly.

"How do you like that, you fucking scab!" yells Tommy, grabbing another handful. "Are you happy you came here, so your big engineer Dad could take people's jobs? Are you?" He crushes the snow into Harry's face.

"Stop!" I scream, lurching toward them. Ange grabs my sleeve, and I feel the cheap vinyl rip.

Bill grabs Tommy's arms. "Come on man, he's had enough. Let him go." The other guy helps Bill pull Tommy off.

Tommy shrugs roughly and walks off, down into the ravine toward where we were sitting, not looking back.

There is no sound from Harry now. We stare for a few moments at the still form before us.

"C'mon kid, it's over," says Bill.

Harry doesn't move.

"No way," says the third guy, staring. "Nobody dies from a goddamn face wash."

"No way," repeats Bill, then more insistently, "Hey!" He leans forward and prods Harry's shoulder.

I blink, feeling like I'm dreaming, as Bill brushes the snow off Harry's face. Harry's skin has gone the oddest colour, a deep grayish-blue.

Harry sits up and opens his eyes.

Except it's not Harry, at least not like he was before. This Harry looks like a photo negative. His hair is completely white, even when the snow has fallen away. The dark part of his eyes is white too, shining, and the white part of his eyes is black. As I stare, this strange anti-Harry stands up and looks at us through the curtain of falling snow.

"What's wrong?" I whisper. All I can think is, he's dead. He's dead or a zombie or something and it's our fault.

Ange gasps, and Harry turns toward her. Before any of us can move, he steps toward her and touches her face. She screams, clutching at her cheek.

Her scream makes my stomach turn liquid. The boys run away in all directions while I stay rooted, unable to move. Ange, Bill and I are the only ones left with Harry. Ange is holding her face in her hands.

"Jesus, what have you done to her?" yells Bill.

Harry looks down at his gray-blue hands as if puzzled and then turns toward Bill, reaching out. His hand stops before touching Bill, but Bill cries out and puts his hands over his eyes.

"I can't see!" Bill lifts his hands away and I see his eyes have gone negative — the whites of them dark, the iris pale. "They burn!" he wails.

I unfreeze and stumble off down the hill, gagging and shivering. I reach the place where we were sitting under the pine tree. Tommy is there, sipping on a beer. He looks up at me.

"What do you want?" he asks. But he is not looking at me. I turn and gasp to see Harry a few feet away.

Harry looks at Tommy and does not respond.

I realize the voices are back, all around me. I don't see Ange and Bill or any of the others, but as I squint through the snow I see more negative figures, moving in from the forest. One of them comes close to me, a female with dark hair, dark gray-blue skin, and white-dark eyes. Disbelieving, I recognize her. The girl who went missing.

"Jane?" I stammer.

"You'd better go," she says. Her voice sounds surprisingly normal.

I turn and see that Tommy has passed out, lying face up on the ground, and Harry is bending over him.

"Don't hurt him!" I plead instinctively.

Harry looks up at me, his strange eyes glowing. I shouldn't have said anything. Tommy started all this, but I can't help feeling sorry for him as he lies there helpless.

Jane puts her hand out, not quite touching my shoulder. I can feel a kind of burn from her hand, right through my jacket.

"You'd better leave," she says. "Or you won't be able to."

I back away. All the figures are closer now, a semi-circle around Tommy and I and Harry and Jane. I'm afraid someone will run forward and grab me, but I manage to back out of range.

Once clear, I yell back, "He didn't mean anything! His dad's always drunk since he lost his job. He hits him!"

There is no reply, but a few of the anti-people turn and watch me. Their eyes frighten me. I run away through the snow.

Norm's Game

Kathy Stinson

I have to laugh. It's impossible not to. My uncle's shorts are soaked all down the front. He's brandishing his fork, grinning, and searching round the table for the one who got him.

"What happened?" Shawna asks me. This is her first time visiting my family's cottage.

"The Water Trick. Usually it gets played on visitors. I'm surprised you aren't the one with the wet lap."

"Norm," Aunt Joan says, "I don't think anyone's ever got you with that trick in all the years we've been married."

"Or when we were kids either," another aunt pipes in.

Uncle Norm is great. Funny, smart, the kind of guy everyone likes to be around. If he's building a deck or painting a cabin, everybody wants to be part of his crew. If it's too cold for swimming, Uncle Norm organizes a badminton or rummy tournament and everybody wants in. But the undignified wet splotch across the front of his shorts is just too funny.

Down the table, Uncle Phil's eyes are laughing as he bites back a smile. Norm laughs. "Point for you, Phil," he says.

"Elaine, I still don't get what happened," Shawna says.

To show her, I fold up the hanging-down edge of the plastic tablecloth in front of me so it makes a trough. "Now you do it."

Beside me Shawna flips up her edge and the trough grows longer.

"Now, if I were to pour this glass of water . . ." I say, "people along the table either catch on and make the trough, and therefore the water, go past them. O-or . . ."

"So, your Uncle Norm didn't catch on."

"Right."

"Why don't we do it now," Shawna whispers, "while everyone's distracted?"

Beside Shawna, Aunt Gloria is reaching for a second bun. "Mm, I really like Aunt Gloria," I say over the chatter and clatter, "but she doesn't take practical jokes very well. Right, Aunt Gloria?"

"That's right."

Phil is refilling his water glass and offering the jug to Norm. It's hard to hear what Gloria is saying over the groans and laughter, but I think it was something to do with some dunking accident she'd rather not talk about. Uncle Norm, oblivious to our conversation, laughs again and tops up his glass, too.

"Are there any more carrots?" Aunt Joan asks.

Someone down the table says, "Could you please pass the gravy?"

Early evening light filters through birch and pine into the screened-in verandah.

"Looks like a nice night for badminton."

"Phil, look out!" Aunt Gloria yells.

Phil pushes away from the table in time. A river of water puddles onto the floor.

Norm wags a finger at Gloria. "Spoilsport! Now I'll have to water-trick you, too!" He refills his glass and makes a big show of taking a small sip.

"You can't," I say. "She's on the wrong side of the table."

For a second I think Norm's going to fling the glass of water right across the table at Gloria — or me — but he pitches it through the screen behind him instead. And everyone laughs.

Except Gloria. She just smiles like she knows she should think this stuff is funny.

"Isn't Gloria Phil's wife?" Shawna asks, still trying to sort out how all my relatives are connected.

"Yeah." I slather more sour cream on my baked potato.

"Then why wouldn't she warn him about the water? Why's your uncle so mad?"

"Oh, he's not really mad. He's just pretending."

Uncle Phil goes into the kitchen, comes back with a jug of water, and sets it in the middle of the table.

"Now, boys," one of the Old Aunts says, "you're taking this too far." There's more laughter then, because someone at the cottage is always being accused of taking something too far.

Phil says, "I just thought people might still be thirsty." More laughter.

Later, when we're clearing the table, the jug disappears from the dining room and from the kitchen. My cousin Garrett walks by the pantry window with a bucket.

Uncle Norm passes through the knot of people starting dishes. "We're going to get you, Gloria."

"What did I do?" she says. "Phil's the one who water-tricked you."

"And you butted in when I could have got him back."

My cousins and I leave our dishtowels and follow Norm out the screen door. Soon only Phil, Gloria and the two Old Aunts are left doing dishes.

Pots, jugs, buckets and a kettle — all snuck from the kitchen and back room while the table was being cleared — are gathered by the tap near the back corner of the cottage. "Most of you should stay near the kitchen door," Norm says, "so she'll think she can sneak out somewhere else. But if she does . . ." Into the bushes he hurls a bucket of water in a splendid silver arc.

The kitchen door opens. Too soon. We're not ready.

But it's only Uncle Phil, heading into the woods. To the outhouse, probably, or maybe to his cabin for a smoke.

"Lisa, Don, you two go round to the front door. Shawna, Bob, you cover the door out the side."

"Why would she go that way?"

"Why does Gloria do anything?"

"How about the roof?" Josh hoists himself to a low section and Norm hands him up a full bucket. Josh carries it to a strategic spot above one of the doors.

"Good idea." Garrett climbs up to cover the kitchen door from above.

Norm hands me a saucepan. "You on my team, kid?"

"Yup."

"I knew I could count on you."

Water from the outdoor tap blasts into my saucepan. My team? It's not even a thought, really. Just a wisp of an idea that puffs through my mind like milkweed fluff on the wind. Is there actually another team? Or is the other team just Gloria?

"Come on out, Gloria," someone calls. "We're going over for badminton."

"Yeah, Gloria," I join in, "come on out."

Gloria answers calmly, "After the dishes," as if she doesn't know how many people with jugs, saucepans and buckets are waiting to douse her as soon as she appears.

"This is taking too long," Garrett says.

"We can wait."

"No we can't."

"Come on, Gloria," Uncle Norm says. "The Old Aunts don't mind finishing those dishes. Let's go play badminton."

Shawna and my cousin Bob wander by the kitchen with racquets. "Elaine, I'm going over now," Shawna says. "It's too perfect a night for badminton to waste it waiting to throw water on someone."

"You don't get it," I say. "It's going to be — "

"No," Shawna says, "I guess I don't."

The sun, shining low through the trees, glistens on the droplets of water clinging to the screen of the empty verandah.

From the roof Josh says, "Maybe she's not coming out."

"She has to come out eventually."

Squatting behind the old birch stump partway up the hill, I shift to take the pressure off my knees, careful not to spill from my saucepan. The kitchen door squeaks open.

Everyone lurches toward it. The Old Aunts come out of the cottage and amble off in the direction of their cabin.

But Gloria doesn't appear. She is prepared, it seems, to wait us out.

Darn. Shawna was right. It is a perfect night for badminton. No wind. Not too hot. And dinner didn't go too late. This waiting is becoming a definite bore.

Intent now on getting over to the court, I dump the water from my saucepan, put it away and grab a racquet from the old umbrella stand in the living room. On my way out of the kitchen Norm sees me with my racquet. "I never took you for a quitter," he says. In Norm's books there's almost nothing worse.

"Gloria's not even in the kitchen anymore," I say. "She must be hiding." I hate how Norm is looking at me. It's like I've been kicked off the winning team. I wish I could rewind like a video and put the racquet back in the cottage and the water back in my saucepan.

"Come on then, let's get her out." Norm starts to pound on the back wall of the cottage. Thump! Thump! "If you're sure you're not a quitter." Thump! Thump! Thump!

It's my way back in. I make a fist and start pounding. Norm hollers, matching each word to a connection of fist and wood, "Come out! Come out!" I drop my badminton racquet on the deck and pound with both fists. Others join in, "Come out! Come out!" and the thumping on the walls and roof of the cottage is like when everyone at school is stomping on the bleachers and the centre's charging down the court to make a basket.

Still no Gloria.

"Go in and find her!" Norm yells. "We'll make her come out!" His fists pound faster, harder. A couple of people dash into the cottage. "We'll put her in the lake!" A bunch of people laugh. Someone starts a chant, "Lake! Lake! Lake!"

I head inside to help flush Aunt Gloria out. It's always hilarious when someone gets dunked. And I am not a quitter.

In the kitchen, I lift the tablecloth on the little table. Aunt Gloria read me a book once when I was little, where a girl hid under a table behind a long tablecloth and eavesdropped on the grown-ups.

But Gloria isn't there.

"Get her! Get Gloria!" the guards outside yell. "Get her! Get Gloria!" Others continue to yell, "Lake! Lake! Lake!" Even in the dim living room in the heart of the cottage, the shouting is loud. The banging shakes the floor and walls. Too bad Shawna's not here for this. For sure she'd get the fun of it now.

I'm determined to find Gloria anyway — for Uncle Norm.

Could she be hiding behind the big chair where the dogs always sleep? No. In the cubby beside the raincoats? It's dark and cobwebby and something in there smells. I feel my way in anyway, but she's not there.

Lisa comes out of the front room where Gloria's kids keep their stuff. "Not in there," she says, and heads into a storage room.

I open the door to Aunt Ada's room. She's not at the cottage this weekend; she's still recovering from a broken hip. It's dark in the room with the curtains pulled, and a bit musty. I stand in the doorway long enough for my eyes to adjust. Nothing here but Ada's old trunk, a chest of drawers and her bed, made up with the Arctic sleeping bag she needs to keep her frail old body warm. I lift the lid of the trunk.

Silly. A person would suffocate in there. Besides, it's full of scrapbooks and blankets. I head out of the room. Gloria's not in here and I've got to find her. Behind me there's something — not exactly a sound, but something that makes me turn back.

I move closer to the bed. I flip down the top edge of the sleeping bag. I open my mouth to shout, I found her! But except in movies I've never seen a grown-up looking terrified before. A vein in Gloria's neck is throbbing. She is staring right at me. Sweat shines on her face and trickles down her temple.

Thump, thump, thump! Norm's voice penetrates the cottage. "Chocolate bar to whoever finds her!" Thump, thump, thump, thump, thump! "An extra big one to whoever gets her in the lake!" Someone laughs. "And then?!" The pitch of Norm's voice is climbing. "We won't let her out!!" Something gravelly catches in the back of his throat. Like he's as mad as Gloria is scared. And no one is pretending now.

But he can't be talking about drowning Aunt Gloria. His cousin's wife? Just because she sabotaged the Water Trick!?

Of course not, it's all just part of the game — the banging and the threats. Part of the fun. And now I've found the prize, I have to tell. It's part of the game.

Gloria is still lying there. She hasn't spoken. She hasn't begged me to keep her hiding place secret. That's what should be happening now. If the game was going how it's supposed to. *Sh, don't tell, quick turn around pretend you didn't see me.*

"Out! Out! Out! Out!"

But Gloria, stiff and silent in the bed, isn't playing. Her eyes are closed now, as if she's taking herself in her mind somewhere far away. Or maybe she's just resigned to her fate.

Behind me doors bang open and shut, furniture scrapes the floor. Outside, the chanting and the thumping continues. All I have to do is shout, *Here she is!* and everyone will come running. Someone will drag Aunt Gloria from the bed. Uncle Norm will squeeze me around the shoulders, shake me and say, *Way to go, kid!* Someone will carry Gloria down to the dock. Will she hang limp or struggle? Either way, everyone will follow them down to the water. Either way, Gloria won't escape. And when she goes in — one, two, three, splash — the laughter will explode and bounce off the cliff on the other side of our bay. Gloria will sink at first, then rise, sputtering. Won't she. She'll drag herself up onto the dock, dripping wet. It'll be hilarious. A scream. A riot. *You're right, Elaine. I don't get it.*

"Not in there!" I hear myself chirp, pulling shut the door. I hope no one picked up a false note in my voice. But who would? My family is like a frenzied pack. How have they come to this? How have I?

I go through the motions of looking in the corner by the bookshelf, but it's hard now even to pretend. I step out of the dim cottage into the clear light of evening.

Sweat is trickling down the side of Uncle Norm's face. His eyes are bright, his cheeks red. He laughs when he sees me. "No luck, eh, kid? Not to worry. You gave it your best."

I pick up the racquet from the deck. "I'm heading over to the court before it gets too dark."

"Why don't we all do that?" he says, and it's like he's given the signal. Norm's game is over. Soon everyone is trailing away from the cottage. Loud enough for Gloria to hear, though, Norm shouts, "Oh well, there's always tomorrow. She can't hide forever." And everyone laughs.

It's almost like normal at the badminton court, with spectators waiting to play crammed onto the log bench Norm helped a bunch of us build or on the ground in front, with players on the east side of the court complaining about the sun. As Norm calls out, "Good shot, Shawna," and "Lovely serve!" it's almost possible to pretend that nothing has happened, nothing has changed. To imagine that tomorrow Norm will want someone to help him carry wood and I'll volunteer, that there'll be a rummy tournament this weekend and I'll be glad if I'm at his table.

There's a movement in the trees and Aunt Gloria, smiling, emerges with Uncle Phil from the woods. Is she trying to pretend, too, that nothing is changed by what happened tonight?

Shawna, just finished her game, hands a racquet to Gloria. But no one steps forward to be her partner. It's like we're all waiting for something. Something from Norm.

A slight breeze drifts through the pines. A motorboat cruises down the lake toward town. Norm twirls a pine needle between his thumb and forefinger.

I stand up and brush sand from the seat of my shorts. "I'll play."

Penance

Cathy Beveridge

" Is that everything, son?"

The voice squeezes through the mesh directly in front of Benjamin, who traces and retraces the shape of a cross on the rail in front of him. In the darkness, his eyes drop to his knees embedded in cold, cranberry leather. "No," comes his breathless reply. "There's one more thing."

"Go ahead."

The voice waits silently as Benjamin summons his courage. "I want to kill my sister."

There is a momentary pause. "I see — an older sister or a younger sister?"

"Uh, older," he stammers. "She's nine."

"And you wish to kill her."

"Yes . . . I mean no, well, yes, I said I did, but I don't, except sometimes when . . . yes." Benjamin presses his fingertips together in the darkness. "Yes," he reconfirms.

"Are you referring then to murder?"

Benjamin draws his tongue along the hard enamel of his teeth. "Murder," he whispers, his eyes wide and awful.

"That is what you had in mind then."

Benjamin is speechless.

"Do you often plot to murder, my son?"

"No!" Defiance bursts from Benjamin's voice, but immediately his tone softens. "No," he whispers. "Just once, once in awhile — and just Angie — my sister."

"Nobody else?"

"No, never!"

"Have you been taught anything about killing — either at home or at school?"

Benjamin rocks from one knee to the other. Again he nods towards the invisible voice. Air escapes noisily from his parched lips. "Yes, that it's wrong, it's a sin." He swallows. "Murderers go to . . . " His voice disappears.

"Go to . . . ?"

Benjamin mouths the dreaded word. Inhaling deeply, he closes his eyes, faces the mesh and speaks, his voice cracking under the weight of his words. "They go to hell."

"Hell?"

Benjamin agrees mutely.

"And exactly where is hell?"

The boy's eyes widen. "At the centre of the earth," he manages.

"And what's it like?"

Tiny drops of sweat cling to the boy's forehead and begin to trickle down his brow. "It's, it's hot."

"Hot?"

"Hot, like a fire, a huge fire."

"There are flames?"

Benjamin nods. "In pits, in the sky, in the water."

"Are there people?"

Benjamin's ankles cross and uncross behind his back. His voice trembles. "Yes, they are there too, in the flames." The boy's blond hair mats against his temples.

"Tell me," the voice says kindly, "when you kill your sister, just how will you do it?"

Benjamin's head jerks upwards. "Do it?"

"Yes, you know, what method of killing will you use — strangulation, drowning, stabbing?"

"Poison!" The word echoes inside the cabinet.

"Ah, poison — arsenic or perhaps cyanide?"

Confusion spreads across the boy's face. "Poison ivy."

"Of course." The voice pauses, coughs and resumes. "And how will you administer the poison?"

"Administer?"

"Yes, how will you go about giving this poison to your sister?"

Benjamin exhales slowly. "I have a plan," he says timidly. The voice's silence indicates that he should continue. "My friend Jeff and I found this patch of poison ivy in the field near Jeff's place. We know for sure it's poison ivy 'cause Jeff's dad was with us when we saw it. He said we weren't to touch it 'cause it can poison you right through your skin."

"So you'll poison your sister by . . . Exactly how does your plan work?"

"Well, you have to know my sister. She's always spying on me and following me around. Anyway, if you want to make sure she knows about something, you just tell her it's a secret. Jeff and me, we're going to take pennies and pretend that we found them in the field."

"But what do pennies have to do with poison ivy?"

Benjamin explains patiently. "Well, my sister's not stupid, see? She's not just going to march into a patch of poison ivy. She doesn't even know where it is. So I figure that me and Jeff have to convince her that we have a secret."

"She's interested in your secrets."

"Uh-huh, but she's more interested in my money."

"Hmm."

"That's why the secret has to have money in it."

"And what exactly is the secret?"

"That we've found a stash of coins, kind of like a buried treasure." Again the silence signals that he is to continue. "We haven't really — I mean we take the pennies with us. But Jeff and me, we'll start making maps and leaving clues in the field."

"Clues?"

"Yeah, spray-painted arrows and pieces of wool tied to plants, stuff like that. Eventually, we'll lead her closer and closer to the poison ivy patch."

"So then she'll follow your trail into the poison ivy patch and be . . . "

" . . . poisoned."

"And then she'll . . . "

" . . . die."

The voice is thoughtful. "So why haven't you gone ahead with your plan?"

Benjamin's palms slap the wooden rail carelessly. "Pennies," he states simply. "I need pennies, but Angie gets them all."

"All of them? Don't you ever get money for helping around the house?"

"Nope. Mom and Dad say that we should help just because we're a family and families have to help each other."

The voice smiles. "Well then, how does your sister get her money?"

"She goes through the laundry to see if Dad's left any change in his pockets."

"And he does?"

"Yep, and I'm supposed to get the pennies. All the change is supposed to go into a jar and at the end of the week, I'm supposed to get the pennies, Angie gets the nickels, and Mom and Dad keep the rest. But Angie always sneaks down and takes all the change before Mom does the wash."

"She must have quite the piggy bank full by now," the voice observes coolly.

"She hides it from Mom and Dad. And then she lies."

"Hmm. And when do you expect to have enough pennies to murder your sister?"

Benjamin winces at the mention of "murder". "Well, maybe I won't exactly murder her," he ponders aloud. "Maybe I'll just let her set one foot in the patch so she just gets real sick." He purses his lips and glances down at the outline of his now-still fingers. "I don't really want to kill her," he admits finally. "I guess I'm sorry I said I did."

❧ ❧ ❧

Benjamin opens his eyes as he finishes making the sign of the cross. He glances around to where Angie is standing in front of the candles, scraping wax drippings into the flames. Benjamin rises to his feet and his sister immediately strides towards him, her dark pigtails bouncing behind her. "Did you tell him what you said about me?" she hisses.

Benjamin scowls but nods.

"So what did he say? Will you go down there?" Angie points to the floor but her brother does not answer. "How much penance did you get?" Benjamin does not reply. "I bet you got more than I did. That's because I don't go around saying I want to kill people."

"Three 'Hail Marys' and two 'Our Fathers'," interrupts Benjamin as their mother approaches.

"But that's all I got." Angie frowns then turns to face her mother. "Mom, how come — "

"Are you leaving Mrs. Fedor?" The children turn towards Father Greg who has come up noiselessly behind them. He places his hands gently on their shoulders as they move towards the door and out into the sunshine. "The collection's all counted and locked in the safe. I gave the totals to Sister Anne," says Benjamin's mother.

"Many thanks." Father Greg looks down at Angie and Benjamin. Angie smiles broadly up at him while Benjamin digs his right shoe into a nearby flowerbed. "I'll see you all on Sunday." He inclines his head towards Mrs. Fedor and pats the children's shoulders. The three move down the stairs.

"Benjamin." The boy turns back towards the man who stands framed in the doorway. The wrinkled hand beckons and dutifully Benjamin returns to the arched entrance of the brick building. "I thought you might be able to find a use for these," Father Greg says, softly cupping the boy's hand in his own. Smiling, he disappears into the cool shadows.

Three copper pennies sparkle in Benjamin's outstretched hand.

Snow and Apples

Lena Coakley

We had played many a small town that season, but this one was hardly more than a tavern and a church with a little bit of dirt road in between. We stopped our horses and cart in a field beside the tavern. Tiny and Mrs. Tiny began to drum up a crowd as they always did, riding around on the shoulders of Ezekiel the Strongman.

"See the tumbling and feats of strength," Ezekiel boomed. "See the very dangerous wild man!"

Slowly a few people began to gather, stamping and blowing on their hands in the chill of the autumn afternoon, but it was hard to get people out of doors in that cold.

Mrs. Tiny had Ezekiel walk right up to the tavern window. "Beautiful women! See the beautiful women!" she shouted, knocking on the shutters. That got the tavern patrons to leave their ale.

Finally, Mrs. Tiny reached into one of her many red pockets and threw a handful of coloured paper into the air. It was the signal to the rest of us that the crowd was large enough and the show should begin.

Millie came first from behind the cart, pretty as a daisy with ribbons at her waist, dressed up as the queen of May. She was the "beautiful women". At home she was plain as butter and shy as a whisper, but Mrs. Tiny could work a kind of magic with the grease paint, and when Millie performed she could toss her skirts and flutter her eyelashes in a way she would never dare any other time.

From the other side of the cart came John and Samkin doing their tumbling and cartwheels to the applause of the onlookers. Most think they must be the children of Tiny and Mrs., because they are small people as well, but really it is Joseph who is their son. Joseph is just as tall as I am. He did not like to be in the show, but stood in the crowd applauding and laughing in all the right places.

Ezekiel helped Mrs. Tiny to the ground. The people in the back craned their necks to see her. "Good ladies and gentlemen," she said smiling widely, all red skirts and red cheeks, "we have entertained lords and noble folk all over the land, and now, with your permission, we shall entertain you."

The crowd shouted and applauded as Mrs. Tiny introduced the members of the company one by one. But she did not introduce me. I was the surprise, the grand finale. I was in the large wooden cage that sat, covered with a black cloth, on the flat bed of the cart. I was dressed in animal skins and covered with blue dye. I am the very dangerous wild man.

Even though I had seen it a hundred times, I loved to watch the show, although I had to lie on the floor of my cage and peer out of a hole in the black cloth in order to see it. Even then I couldn't make out everything. Ezekiel performed his feats of strength right before I was supposed to go on. He held up a bar with John and Samkin holding on to one end, Tiny and Mrs. Tiny dangling from the other. Then Millie propped a little ladder against his back, climbed up and stood on his shoulders. The people hooted and laughed at this bit even without Joseph's prompting. They were a good crowd and the Lord knows they could do with a good time before the winter set in. I just hoped that Millie's sack would be full of coins and not buttons and carrot ends like we'd had in the last town.

In spite of the cold I was sweating in my animal skins, but I was looking forward to my bit. When I heard Mrs. Tiny's voice saying, "and now, Good Folk, we must take our leave," I was disappointed not to get my chance to perform. A moment later, Millie shoved the sack between the curtains. Only one or two coins jingled at the bottom and something else, hard and round, a stone I thought. "What's wrong, Millie?" I asked. "I haven't done my part." But I could see that the stutters had stopped up her tongue and I didn't press. I hid the money sack under a lump of hay in my cage and the cart lurched so quickly to a start that I lost my balance and hit my head against the bars. I could hear Joseph using the whip on Blackie and Brownie, something he hardly ever did. He was tender-hearted and loved those horses.

After a time the cart slowed, and since we were away from the town I felt it was safe to open the black curtains at the back and ask someone what was going on. The little ones and Millie usually rode up front, but Ezekiel was at the back of the cart clinging to the bars of the cage.

"The Viscount's men," said the Strongman bending to speak to me. "They were in the crowd."

"The Viscount as well?"

"Couldn't see, but Tiny thinks we had better go home for a while until they find that nobleman's daughter."

A bald head appeared upside down from above. Samkin had been riding on the top of the cage. "They'll never find her. Most likely she's fallen down a well or been murdered by her own family. No use looking, I say." Samkin was never one for looking on the bright side.

"Perhaps she has eloped with her peasant love." The hem of a blue skirt and a pair of brown shoes appeared before me as Millie sat down on the roof, dangling her legs over the edge. Now that the danger was past and it was just ourselves, her stutters had disappeared.

"What a notion!" Samkin snorted. "Rich women don't marry peasants. And her father's richer than the Viscount, so they say."

"Rich and beautiful too," said Millie, "what would you give for that, Ezekiel?"

"Better to say your prayers and save your soul," said Ezekiel, who was the most pious among us.

"Father Collier once told me that a perfectly beautiful person would have a soul as white as snow," I said, "because beauty is an outward sign of God's favour. He said that beauty was God's voice saying: 'here is where true goodness lies.'"

I saw Ezekiel and Samkin exchange a glance and there was an awkward silence as Millie's scuffed brown shoes banged gently against the bars of my cage. I was sorry to have made my friends uncomfortable. Father Collier was not a cruel man, but until that moment I had not thought what his words meant about those who were not beautiful. I had not wondered what God's voice was saying about me through my misshapen face.

"Doesn't matter where she is," said Ezekiel, changing the subject. "The Viscount will use her disappearance as an excuse to search every traveller on the road, and relieve them of their gold while he's at it. The man's no better than a highwayman."

They say that too much talking about evil is likely to bring it about, and in this case it proved true for suddenly the cart gave another lurch and I was pitched again, this time to the other end of my cage, as we came to a halt.

"You'll be tending my bruises tonight, Joseph," I yelled, but Ezekiel hushed me quiet and shut my curtains again.

"Halt and prepare to be searched," a male voice called. I peered out through a gap in the black fabric and saw that six or seven horsemen surrounded us.

Mrs. Tiny jumped from the cart, her red flannel skirt billowing around her. "We are honest folk," she said to the man who had spoken. "We have nothing to hide."

"You haven't seen a girl then," someone asked, a different rider this time with a softer voice. "A young gentlewoman is missing. I'm sure you will want to help us find her." I angled myself so that I could see this new speaker. He was a young man, no older than I. He rode a gray stallion and was himself clothed all in dove gray. The white feather in his cap was held with a diamond pin, or what I took to be a diamond, and his gray riding boots were of such a soft leather I was sure they would be ruined if they touched the ground.

Mrs. Tiny looked squarely up at the man although she must have known he was the Viscount himself. "There are no gentlefolk among us."

The man laughed and a great guffaw went up from the horseman. "That," said the Viscount smirking, "we can clearly see. However, the cost of conducting a search for the poor lady is very high. We are asking honest citizens like yourselves for contributions." The Viscount paused to stroke the neck of his beautiful horse. "My men tell me you have a small sack of coins. This is just the sort of thing we are looking for. Men," he called, "search the cart."

I pulled back from the curtain in alarm, looking for a better place to hide our money, but the only things in the cage besides the pile of hay were a few large ox bones that I used in my act. I was at a loss for what to do until I heard Mrs. Tiny say in a loud voice, "Perhaps it is not wise to awaken the beast." I had heard those words so many times before that I lost my fear in a moment.

"He is a wild man with a taste for human flesh," said Ezekiel in the same loud stage voice. I grabbed one of the bones from the corner of the cage and waited. Ezekiel pulled the rope that dropped the black curtain and I stood blinking in the bright light of day.

"He is awake!" shouted Mrs. Tiny, clutching her head with her hands. Millie let out a long, high-pitched scream that made the horses rattle in their trappings (all except Blackie and Brownie of course who were used to it). I began to hit the wooden bars of the cage with my bone. Tiny, John, Joseph and Samkin ran about yelling, "oh no," and, "Lord preserve us," and causing general chaos. At just the right moment I stepped back a few paces and then made a running leap at the cage bars, or rather I made a running leap at one particular bar, the one Tiny had sawn through at the top so that it would break easily.

"ARRRRGH!" I growled and broke free, swinging my bone in a wide circle. Millie screamed again and fell down in a mock faint. "Give me meat!" I cried.

Normally Ezekiel would have done his strongman act at this point, forcing me into submission to the applause of the crowd, but this time the wild man was not so easily beaten. I tore at my hair. I beat the ground with my bone. But this is what made the Viscount and his men turn their horses and run: I made sure each one of them saw my face. Because there is something about my face, something you can't put on with just blue dye and animal skins, something gone wrong.

It has been said that even my mother could not look at me, though I have never met the woman and cannot say if this is true. The flesh above my lip is torn, separated, so that even when my mouth is closed, my teeth show through. She left me on the steps of a church. The priest who found me let me live there, as no one else would take me in. I had once thought of becoming a priest myself. But Father Collier made me see as kindly as he could that this would never happen. I left when I was fifteen, so as not to be a burden on him any longer.

I changed my clothes in the cage after we crossed the river, and rubbed off as much of the blue dye as I could. Then, to give the horses a rest, we walked the last miles to the cottage. There was much laughing and clapping me on the back along the way.

"Best performance you've ever given, Tom," said Ezekiel.

"Aye, now when the Mrs. says we've performed for noble folk she won't be telling a lie," said Tiny.

"All that for three brass coins and an acorn," said Samkin with his nose in the money sack. "Oh wait. This too." Samkin reached into the sack and drew out a round apple — such a perfect thing, and rosy. It was decided that I should have it, although I thought it should have gone to Mrs. Tiny, and I put it in my pocket.

"What is it, Joseph?" said John.

Joseph stood with his hand shading his eyes. "There's smoke coming out of our chimney."

You will have read other things about her and I will tell you now that they are all lies, all except this, the one kernel of truth at the heart of the story: she truly was as beautiful as a drop of blood in the snow. When I first saw the Mistress Clare my breath clotted in my chest, my ears rang and I was stung with beauty.

As we came up to the cottage she burst coughing out of the door, billows of smoke following after. She ran right into me in her haste, but she didn't scream. She put her hand over her mouth and looked at us one to the other. I thought for a moment she had begun to cry from fear, but a moment later I saw that she was laughing.

"Now I understand why the chairs are so small," she said.

"Wh . . . wh . . . what is burning?" Millie cried pushing past her, but the girl seemed unconcerned.

"Oh, the beastly fire wouldn't start. I think your fireplace is broken." Samkin went in to help Millie while the rest of us stayed outside gaping at the young noblewoman.

Finally Mrs. Tiny spoke. "You've run away, I suppose."

"Yes."

"Your father and mother are looking for you."

"My father and stepmother you mean, and I don't suppose that they are looking very hard."

"But they are," I sputtered, "After losing you they are searching the ends of the earth. They do not stop even to rest!" I did not know the girl's parents of course, but how could they do otherwise?

Mrs. Tiny sighed and raised an eyebrow in my direction. When she spoke she sounded tired. "Tom, take the lady into the garden. If we're to have a noblewoman as a guest we have a lot of work to do before nightfall."

Samkin poked his head out of the window. "It's all right in here. Girl forgot to open the flue."

And so it was that I got to spend an hour with perfect beauty. Tucked in behind the house, our garden has always been my favourite place. It was autumn now, but I described to her what it was like in the spring with the rows of new shoots curling out of the ground. She told me about her stepmother.

"Does she really treat you as a servant?" I asked, thinking of the job she had made of lighting the fire.

"Oh yes," she said, "and I am beaten most every night. Also, I am forced to wear dresses of rags . . . except for this one," she said quickly. "This is the dress I wear when I am in my father's presence."

"It's lovely," I said. The blue fabric changed in the light like the wings of a butterfly.

"It was torn in the woods." Clare showed me a tear at the bottom of her skirt. "You are torn as well." She reached out and ran her finger over the jagged cleft between my nose and lip. I blushed and pulled away.

"They say that is where the Lord touches us before we are born. I suppose he must have struck me."

"Oh no, he wouldn't do that," she said. "A tiny baby not even born, what could you have done wrong?"

It brought a tear to my eye her saying that. It seemed like the kindest thing anyone had ever said to me. I reached into my pocket and brought out the perfect apple. She smiled gratefully and took a bite.

"Quick! They've found us!" John tugged at the bottom of my jacket.

"What?"

"Ezekiel says there are riders on the road — the Viscount and his men. And the girl's father is with them this time."

Mrs. Tiny ran into the garden followed by Millie carrying our moneybox. Mrs. Tiny began to dig with her hands into a patch of garden.

"Where shall I hide?" asked the mistress Clare.

"There's no time to dig," said Millie.

"Where shall I hide!?"

"We'll throw the money into the well," said Mrs. Tiny. "Worry about how to get it out later."

Joseph and Tiny came from around the barn leading Blackie and Brownie.

"I'm damned if the Viscount will have you," Joseph cried, and he rapped the horses on the rump with a stick. The two horses cantered off into the trees.

"You will all listen to me now! You will all listen to me right now!" Clare shouted. We all stopped. "Where will I hide? I will not go back to living with my stepmother." Mrs. Tiny strode over to the noblewoman and glared up at her.

"Girl," she said, "I would rather it be you I was throwing down the well than our money for all the trouble you've caused. We have a cottage with one room and a barn with one room. There is no place where we can hide you that won't be discovered."

"I will tell you, little woman, there had better be someplace, because if my father finds me here I will tell him that you have kidnapped me, and then he will hang you from the tallest tree." There was a long silence and then a crash as Millie dropped the moneybox. Coins poured out into the garden rows. Mrs. Tiny did not take her eyes from the Mistress Clare.

"Tiny," she said to her husband, "go get one of the straw pallets from the house. Millie, pick up that money. And the rest of you, go dab some vinegar in your eyes. Make it look as though you've been crying. Oh, it will be a miracle if we're all alive in an hour."

Just moments later, the seven of us were kneeling around the straw pallet where Mistress Clare lay, pretending to be asleep. Next to me, Millie was shaking like a reed in the wind. I was certain that the Viscount would slaughter us all.

"Are we to be treated to yet another peasant show?" he said as he rode up with his men. "Do you think to fool us twice in one day?"

"Oh do not mock us in our sorrow," said Mrs. Tiny clutching her chest. The Viscount clapped his gloved hands together in imitation of applause, but one man in the party seemed genuinely alarmed.

"Clare," the man cried, quickly dismounting from his horse. He was a sad looking man with the same black hair and pale beauty as the woman lying at his feet.

"Do not touch her!" said Mrs. Tiny. "She is bewitched." The man drew back and a few of the men crossed themselves, but the Viscount only rolled his eyes.

"Are you her father, sir?" Mrs. Tiny asked.

"I am."

Mrs. Tiny pulled out a red handkerchief and dabbed her eyes. "Then let me tell you our sad story."

Mrs. Tiny wove a tale around and around the Mistress Clare's father. She told him of a witch who was jealous of his daughter's beauty. She told him of a poison apple and a dark enchantment. She told him that only the kiss of true love could unlock the spell. I was still certain we would be slaughtered. But the nobleman nodded his head as if seeing the truth of it all.

"Surely you don't believe this . . . fairy tale," said the Viscount.

Mrs. Tiny put her hands on her hips and gave him the same look she gives to her husband when he drops the juggling balls. "Oh," she said still looking directly at him, "If only true love would come to claim his prize with a kiss. His rich prize. His very rich prize."

There was an awkward silence. The Viscount has missed his cue, I thought. Could I . . . ?

"My love!" cried the Viscount dismounting from his horse. He roughly pushed Millie and me aside and knelt before the Mistress Clare.

Our eyes met and I stared at him coldly. "Do you wish you were me, Wild Man?" he whispered. I knelt in the cold dirt and watched as he kissed her. The Mistress Clare raised her head slightly, arched her back to meet his lips.

"It's a miracle!" Mrs. Tiny cried.

The Mistress Clare yawned and stretched charmingly. She would have made an excellent actress. "Oh father," she said. "I heard all that this peasant said as if it were a dream, and she was too modest to tell you a most important part of the story: it was my stepmother who bewitched me. It breaks my heart to tell you." She cast her eyes to the ground.

❧ ❧ ❧

The seven of us stood watching them go in the dying light. Before they went over the hill and out of our lives, the Mistress Clare turned on the back of the Viscount's horse and smiled brilliantly. She raised her hand. "Goodbye my little friends. You will always be remembered."

"Will they burn her?" asked Millie. "The stepmother — now that the Mistress Clare has accused her, will she be burned as a witch, do you think?"

"That only happens to the poor," said Samkin.

Mrs. Tiny shook her head and went into the cottage. One by one, the others left to go about the business of chopping wood or making dinner, until only I was left to stare at the spot where she had disappeared.

I couldn't have kissed her, I thought. It couldn't have been me, and besides, she was a spoiled, wicked thing. But then I remembered the shimmer of her dress, her touch on my face.

A light snow, the first of the season, began to fall. Brownie wandered out of the woods and ambled to my apple, which lay forgotten on the ground. I decided not to stop him from eating it, and turned, finally, towards the glow of our cottage. Perhaps, I thought, I am losing my taste for perfect apples.

The Challenge

Jacqueline Pearce

The griffin screamed then dove, its talons outstretched. Scott held his ground, sword raised. The creature was almost on him, dagger claws inches from his face. Scott swung the sword and stepped clear. The griffin fell, blood spurting from its now headless neck. Scott sheathed his sword and began walking again. He had to get to the mountain, find the hidden treasure and get back to ransom the captive princess. He could see the mountain in the distance, but between it and him lay a wasteland. Desert. His strength level was dropping. The mountain was getting closer, but his strength was almost gone. He had to find something to raise it fast. He stumbled over a rock, almost stepped on a plant. The plant: that was it. It might be poison, but it was his only chance. He ate. His strength level began to rise. Excellent. With renewed energy, he began climbing the mountain. Then he saw the cave entrance. He stepped through into a system of under-ground tunnels and caverns.

⁂

Scott caught up with Derek after school the next day.

"Come over to my place?" he asked. "You gotta see this new game I found."

"Great."

They stepped out of the school building and began to cut across the soccer field. Their runners squelched on the wet grass. Ahead of them, the girls' soccer team was prac-tising.

"Who's that?" Derek asked. A girl wearing black shorts and a white T-shirt splattered with mud was waving at them.

"I don't know. Is she saying something to us?"

Suddenly, a soccer ball landed on the grass in front of them, spraying water.

"Shee-it!"

The girl jogged up.

"Hi Scott, Derek. Thanks for stopping the ball for us." She smiled mockingly, then kicked the ball, sending it flying back across the field.

"See you around."

They watched her jog away — long legs, short shorts, streaming brown hair.

"Shee-it!" Derek said again, under his breath. "Was that Jaimie Fletcher?"

"From grade six? Nah, it couldn't be." Scott remem-bered grade six. Jaimie Fletcher had been plain looking, skinny and taller than he'd been. She'd threatened to beat him up on several occasions. It was hard to tell anything about the mud-splattered girl on the soccer field, but if it was Jaimie Fletcher, she'd definitely gained some curves. Scott felt something stir in his gut. Was it fear or interest?

"So, tell me about this game," Derek said as they started walking again. Scott shook off the unexplained feeling. Yeah, the game. Now, he regretted asking Derek to come over. He wanted to get back into the game by himself. Get to the next level.

⁂

Scott moved through the darkness beneath the mountain. Torches set into the cave walls partially illuminated his passage. Suddenly, he rounded a corner, and two trolls blocked his path. Their heads were huge and ugly, with large dark-vision eyes. One waved a spiked club, the other wore a large green stone around his neck and brandished a crooked dagger. Scott retreated back around the corner. He pulled a torch from the wall and held it out in front of him. The trolls rounded the corner and cringed back from the sudden light, dropping their weapons. On impulse, Scott grabbed the stone from around the second troll's neck, then continued down the tunnel. The trolls did not follow.

Scott moved deeper into the heart of the mountain. Suddenly he came to a junction. Ahead of him, the tunnel opened up into two passages. It was impossible to tell which was the right one. He held up the green stone. It began to glow. Green light flowed out from the stone and fell across the opening of the left tunnel. Scott stepped after it. The treasure was close. He could feel it.

Derek had gone home long ago. Outside Scott's room, rain lashed the window. There was a flash, followed by a boom. Scott didn't look up. Now that he was into the game again, he was determined to keep going until he finished it. Something pressed at the edges of his attention — something he should do. But he pushed the thought away. It could wait.

Suddenly, the room lit up. Then, about the same moment the accompanying boom sounded, the computer screen crackled and went black.

"What the — ?"

Scott pulled his hands away from the keyboard. Then he smelled smoke.

After school the next day, Scott and Derek stepped out onto the back field as usual. Scott shook his head, swearing again as he thought ahead to the dead computer waiting at home.

"God, why didn't I stop and turn it off?" he lamented. He kicked at the grass, ignoring the dampness. There was nothing to hurry home for now. The computer was a write-off, and there was no chance of replacing it any time soon.

"That stupid game," Scott went on. "I was on a roll, too. Nothing could kill me."

"Except the weather," Derek commented.

Scott laughed without humour. Then he noticed Derek was not actually looking at him — had probably not been for some time. Scott turned his head to see what had caught Derek's attention. The girls' soccer team was out on the field again — this time, wearing uniforms. A team from another school was warming up on the opposite end of the field. Derek and Scott were passing near the bleachers by this time. They paused.

"Hey, are you staying for our game?" Jaimie Fletcher called to them as she jogged in front of the bleachers. She kicked a soccer ball lightly from foot to foot, then passed it to another girl who looked vaguely familiar to Scott.

The other girl caught the pass, then looked over at Scott and Derek.

"We could use some cheerleaders," she said, smiling.

Scott felt caught off guard, unsure of how to respond. Video games, computers, he was good at. Joking with girls he was not. Derek did not seem to have this problem. He took on an effeminate pose and shook imaginary pom poms above his head. The girls laughed, glancing back over their shoulders as they ran off.

"Did you see that?" Derek nudged Scott.

"What?"

"Interested females, you idiot!"

"Oh, right. Interested in you — not." But he had to admit, Derek's little act had seemed to impress them somehow. He could never have pulled something like that off, himself. He felt that twinge in his gut again. He shrugged it off.

"Come on. Let's check this out for a minute." Derek jumped up to the middle of the bleachers — with more athletic effort than usual, Scott noted. Reluctantly, Scott climbed up after him.

"That other girl," Derek asked. "Her name's Fiona isn't it?"

"Yeah, I think so," Scott remembered. She'd been in a couple classes with him last year.

As the game got underway, Scott watched without real interest. At least, he told himself he'd rather be at home finishing the game on his computer. But then, that was no longer possible. He swore again and pounded the bench seat.

"Relax, man," Derek said, leaning his elbows back on the seat behind him and stretching his legs out in front. "You got nothing else to do, and this might pay off."

"Yeah, right." Scott was sarcastic.

"You're interested, aren't you?"

Scott shrugged. How could he admit to Derek that girls (and Jaimie Fletcher in particular) made him nervous? He reminded himself that Jaimie was no longer bigger than him, but he suspected that she was even more capable of humiliating him now.

Derek whooped, drawing Scott's attention back to the game. Fiona, on defense, had just taken the ball away from the other team and passed it up the wing to Jaimie. Now Jaimie was running toward the other team's net with a breakaway. Scott leaned forward. Jaimie faked a shot to the goalkeeper's right, then sent the ball deftly into the opposite corner. Off balance, the keeper had no chance. It was a perfect goal. Scott lent his own cheers to Derek's.

Despite himself, Scott actually began to enjoy the game. He had to admit that Jaimie and Fiona were both good players, and watching their bodies move was much more interesting than watching guys play. When the final whistle blew, Scott and Derek were on their feet cheering and whistling. Several girls, including Jaimie and Fiona, looked over at them with appreciation.

Scott and Derek hung around while the girls huddled and did a kind of cheer for the other team, then began to collect their things and leave the field. Jaimie and Fiona waved to their teammates and began walking over to the bleachers.

"Good game!" Scott found himself echoing Derek's words as the two girls walked up. Both girls smiled broadly. Their hair was damp, and Scott could smell their sweat — almost sweet.

"Thanks for staying," Jaimie said, looking at Derek first, then Scott. Had her eyes lingered on Scott's just a little bit longer? Nah, couldn't have.

"Yeah, you guys were great," Fiona added. "I wish more people would come out for our games."

"You were the ones who were great!" Derek said.

"Yeah, it was just as good as watching a guys' game," Scott added.

"Why wouldn't it be?" Jaimie said sharply. Scott cringed inwardly, realizing his mistake too late.

"Hey!" Derek said, changing the subject and wasting no time. "Are you two doing anything Friday night? Do you want to go to a show or something?"

"Oh," Jaimie looked slightly taken aback. Here it comes, Scott thought — the humiliation. "Well, actually I have to babysit Friday night."

Fiona shrugged, looked apologetic. Scott stared out across the field. Three remaining stragglers were just leaving. He wished he was walking away too — wished he was somewhere else other than here by the bleachers.

Jaimie and Fiona had turned to each other.

"What about Saturday?" Fiona whispered.

"Nah, I don't think they're up to it." Jaimie's whisper was obviously calculated to be audible to Scott and Derek. Scott felt his interest perk at the hint of challenge in her words.

"Up to what?" Derek asked, an answering challenge in his voice.

"Well, we were planning to bike the Sea Wall Saturday. Maybe you'd like to come with us — if it's not too much for you."

Derek smiled and turned to Scott. "I don't know. Do you think they could keep up with us?"

Shut up, Scott wanted to say to Derek. Let's get out of this while we can. But he knew it was already too late. If they said "no" they'd look like wimps. But if they tried to ride that distance with these two girls who were obviously in good shape, they'd really end up looking bad. This was definitely a no-win situation.

"I'm willing to let them try," Scott said with a confidence he didn't feel.

"Great! We'll meet you Saturday at the school, then," Jaimie said brightly. Then she met Fiona's eyes with the look of a spider who has got the fly right where she wants it.

That's it, Scott told himself. We're dead.

ᔅ ᔅ ᔅ

Scott rounded a corner in the dark tunnel. Ahead of him was a dead end — nothing but blank rock. He held up the troll's stone. The wall lit up with green light. Then the light faded and only a luminous green outline remained — a door. He pushed the rock door aside and crawled through into a small room. In the centre sat the treasure box.

Scott stirred in his sleep, reached out, rolled over.

Scott clutched the treasure box and began to retrace his steps. Now to save the princess. Tunnel and desert seemed to pass in one step. He was outside the chamber of the princess. The lock fell away from the door, and he entered. The princess stood, her back to him, her long gown dusting the floor and her hair falling in waves down her back. Even without seeing her face, he knew she was beautiful, and that all he wanted was her. Then she turned to meet him. It was Jaimie Fletcher. Suddenly she transformed into a huge giant wearing a muddy soccer uniform. Her smile taunted him. Then she lifted one huge foot and crushed him.

ᶻᵃ ᶻᵃ ᶻᵃ

Scott woke up drenched in sweat, his heart pounding. The dream-Jaimie lingered in his mind like a dangerous and tantalizing ghost. He felt both a sense of anticipation and of dread. It was Saturday.

An hour and a half later Scott and Derek dismounted their bikes in front of the school. Scott removed his helmet, which was feeling too small, and stretched his sweatshirt to wipe his face. God, he was sweating already, and they hadn't even started. He looked around. Maybe the girls wouldn't show. Maybe that was their joke. No such luck. Jaimie and Fiona glided into the parking lot. They could have ridden right out of some cycle magazine. Shiny bikes, all the proper gear — shoes, shorts, gloves, brand new helmets.

"'Morning boys," Jaimie drawled. Both she and Fiona looked fresh and ready to go.

"Ladies." Derek touched his helmet in a salute.

"Hi," Scott said lamely. He wished he had a magic troll's stone or something to help him see a way out of this.

"Do you want to follow us?" Fiona suggested.

"Anywhere you like," Derek replied.

They headed out, Jaimie and Fiona riding side by side in the lead. Derek rode close to Scott, nudging him in the ribs and gesturing appreciatively at the view of the two riders in front. His petal hooked Scott's for a moment, and the two bikes threatened to careen into a parked minivan.

"Watch it!" Scott hissed, jerking his bike free. This was not going to be a good day.

Jaimie and Fiona looked back over their shoulders.

"Coming, guys?" Jaime called, laughter in her voice. Scott hoped she hadn't seen their near mishap.

The four bikes dropped into single file as a moving car passed them. By the time they reached the busy traffic area near False Creek, Scott's thighs were aching, and his butt was sore. *Strength level dropping. Need something to raise it.*

Jaimie and Fiona turned off the busy road onto the wide sidewalk following the edge of False Creek. Then they slowed their pace, dropping back beside Scott and Derek.

"Do you guys need a break?" Fiona asked.

"Not us," Derek answered quickly. Like hell we don't, Scott wanted to say. He wished they'd never started this phony macho stuff, which they now seemed to be stuck keeping up. He tried discreetly to wipe the sweat from his face with his sleeve. Jaimie and Fiona both looked cool and relaxed.

"Do you do this very often?" Scott asked Jaimie, who was riding beside him.

"Once in awhile," she answered. "Do you cycle much?"

"No. Actually, I haven't ridden this bike in months," he answered truthfully.

"I kind of figured that," she said, laughing a little. Scott looked at her face. She didn't seem to be gloating or mocking. He ventured a smile.

As they rode at the more leisurely pace, Scott began to relax and get a bit of a second wind. Maybe he'd make it after all.

"Hey, I think it's going to rain," Fiona announced. Great, that was all Scott needed. He remembered the lightning storm of a few nights ago. He hadn't been having much luck with weather.

They dropped into single file again as Jaimie and Fiona led them back into traffic. Raindrops were beginning to land on Scott's face and bare hands. He could see the green trees of Stanley Park where the Sea Wall started. They just had to make it around the park, then head back to where they'd started from so long ago this morning. "Just" — that was a joke.

On the Sea Wall, Scott found himself riding side by side with Jaimie again. Fiona and Derek rode in front. Snatches of their conversation drifted back with the cold, wet wind. Out on the ocean, whitecaps scudded in under Lion's Gate bridge. Gulls screamed as they flew inland over the Sea Wall.

Suddenly, the sky opened, and rain hit Scott and the others like a wave. The girls' voices echoed those of the gulls. They darted for the cover of a tunnel. In the sheltering dim light Scott leaned his bike against the cement wall and stood by Jaimie. She pulled off her helmet and lifted her face, wet and exhilarated.

"Wow," she said.

Derek and Fiona had set their bikes against the wall too and were huddling together. Outside the tunnel all details had blurred gray behind a wall of falling water.

"Well, I guess my dad could come and pick us up in his van," Jaimie suggested.

"But what about the Sea Wall?" Scott asked, taken aback. He felt off balance. He'd thought the outcome had to be either win or lose. Now, the rules seemed to be changing. Or had he got it wrong all along?

"Don't you want to finish?" he asked, stupidly.

Jaimie shrugged. "We can if you want to." She lowered her eyes, then looked back up at him. "Or we could do something else."

Was she teasing him or was this some kind of proposition? Perhaps it depended on his answer. Ahead of him, the path forked. He had to choose his next step carefully.

Scott looked over at Derek and Fiona. Their heads were together in conversation, oblivious to him. He'd get no help there. He was on his own in new territory. He glanced sideways at Jaimie, hoping to catch a telltale look in her face. She was looking down, her damp hair hanging forward. The Jaimie in this morning's dream leapt into his mind, transforming from beautiful princess into frightening giant. The girl beside him was wet, bedraggled and, at the moment, neither beautiful nor frightening. At least, not exactly. Yet, there was that twist in his gut again. Oh, well, here goes . . . Blindly, he turned to the left passage and stepped ahead.

"Well," Scott stammered. "Something else sounds okay about now." He gestured out at the rain.

Jaimie looked up and smiled. She stepped closer to Scott and reached out to take hold of his arm. He felt suddenly warm on the side of his body next to hers. He'd expected humiliation or victory. Instead, he wasn't sure yet what he'd got. But it was starting to feel good. He stood with Jaimie looking out at the rain, no longer bothered by the chill and dampness. He held no magic troll's stone, he couldn't see what lay ahead, but new possibilities began to open like doors in Scott's mind.

The Merc and Me

Bonnie Dunlop

I'm looking for Katy. Last time I saw her, she was guzzling beer like there was no tomorrow, biting the caps off the bottles to impress her friends.

So far, she hasn't had so much as a chipped tooth, but it makes me shiver to watch her, biting with a quick twist and handing the open beer over with a smile. Although when she's drinking beer, she's almost always smiling.

Right now, she's smiling at Murray, offering him a sip. Surprising, 'cause Katy doesn't share her beer. Makes me wonder if they've got something going. Hard to tell, with Katy.

Somehow, Katy got the car so we could come to the lake. I think she only asks me along in case she gets too drunk to look after herself. I'm the kid sister so how I ended up being her keeper I have no idea. Shouldn't she be the one watching out for me?

We were supposed to be waterskiing today, but that never happened. What happened was they ran out of beer, a real emergency. So Katy took our car and got some more.

We've only got one car and we don't get it often. I don't suppose my dad has any idea that Anne's parents are gone and won't be back 'til Tuesday. If he did, for sure this day would have been out for us.

Now it's time to go. I'm ready, but Katy isn't.

"Come on Katy. We promised we wouldn't be late and it's almost suppertime. We gotta go. Now."

She looks up at me from her perch on a full box of beer. "Chill out, kid. I'm gonna call Dad. Will you get off my case if I call and get the official go-ahead?"

So I promised, although I doubted that even Katy could get around Dad while we still had possession of his precious car.

"Hi, Dad? Yeah, it's me, Katy. Uh-huh, I know we're late. Of course not. Well, maybe just a couple. Oh no, I'm sure I can still drive. Well, if Cindy had her learner's it wouldn't be a problem. Oh, no, don't worry, it'll be fine with them. Okay, okay, I won't. Yup, I promise. And don't worry. We will."

She bangs the receiver down, giving me the thumbs-up. She's gotten us a reprieve, promised Dad we'd be home by 10:00 Sunday, no later, so we'll still have time to make it to church.

After that call, it was all systems go and the party was officially on. I guess the neighbours weren't too impressed, because about 3:00 AM, they called the cops to shut the party down. At the lake, parties are the norm, so if they called the cops on a Saturday night, this one must have gone way over the line.

119

This morning, the lake is calm, dead calm. So is everything else around the cabin, although you couldn't make that statement when the cops showed up.

The sun is rising over the hills, spilling across the lake towards the beach and public campground. On our side, the shade still holds, so it'll be cool for another hour or two.

Those lucky enough to be solidly laid out from last night's beer binge might get another couple hours of dreamless sleep, but not me. I'm looking for Katy.

I've already checked all the rooms, including the can, just in case she was in there horking. God, I have no idea how many beers she downed last night. Her capacity amazes me. Scares me too.

I pick my way across the verandah, littered with empty bottles and full partiers.

Their bodies are curled up for warmth, most of them sleeping where they dropped.

Katy, I see, has at least had the sense to drop on the lounger on the south side of the verandah. Someone even threw an old sweater over her. I wonder who's been taking care of her.

"Come on Katy, it's already eight. You promised Dad we'd be home in time for church. We've gotta stop for gas and by the time we get home, we'll be just under the wire. Now haul ass. You're the one who made the promise."

She snuggles down under the sweater and starts to snore gently. I poke her. No response. I poke her again.

"Get up. Right now."

"Jesus, will you leave me alone? I need water."

Inside the dark and quiet kitchen, I find a clean glass. I bring her the water.

She's dead to the world so I shake her, hard. She groans, rolls over and comes up swinging. If there's one thing Katy really hates, it's someone waking her up before she's ready.

I react, throwing the water into her face. She's spluttering and cursing, throwing more punches.

I'm already running, toward the car. Fumbling with the keys, I jump in and start the engine.

"You better turn that damn car off. We've hardly got enough gas to make it to the service station as it is." She bashes her fist on the hood and glares at me through the windshield.

I shut the car off and wait.

She's checking her jeans, searching in every pocket. I guess she forgot about the beer run. She spent damn near every cent we had.

She'd have spent it all, but I snagged a five and put it in my own pocket. It's almost a miracle I managed to hang onto the fin.

She glares at me.

"You've got some coin I hope."

"Five bucks," I say.

"I'm driving." She opens the door and waits for me to get out. She's quite the sight this morning. Any morning for that matter, but today's worse.

"Okay," she says. "Fork over the cash."

I do it without thinking, pulling the bill from my pocket, holding it in my open palm. She snatches it. In the blink of an eye, the five is gone.

I can't believe my eyes. She's eaten the goddamn thing. She takes about three chews and swallows it. Opens her mouth and shows me.

"Are you nuts?" I screech at her. "Or still drunk?"

She stretches, a big house-cat stretch. Looks at me and grins. "Ha!" she says.

"Gonna have a hell of a time driving home without gas. Maybe we can borrow some money later. No use waking anyone now. They'll just be pissed off. Might as well sleep a little longer."

She heads back to the verandah, anticipating sleep. But she's laughing, digesting the cash and enjoying it at my expense.

There's a phone booth at the corner, so I dig in my pockets, find a dime to call Dad. He is not pleased, to say the least. I tell him we've got a nail in our tire and have to wait 'til noon when the tire guy gets to work. He doesn't believe a word I'm saying, but I lie my face off.

I feel like crying and I'm too damn mad to sleep, so I go into the gloom of the summer kitchen and boil the kettle. I fill the old tin dishpan and wash the dishes. Then I clear the remains of last night's festivities, dumping out the ashtrays, putting the empties back into the cases and wiping the table, sticky with dried booze.

When I'm done, I grab a magazine and sit, tapping my foot on the cool linoleum, wishing it was Katy's head.

I should never have come with her to this stupid party in the first place. I might have known I'd end up babysitting. You'd never know she's two years older than me. She just doesn't give a damn about anything, has no sense of responsibility.

Like today. Why am I the one who has to call home? She just goes to sleep, and lets things work themselves out. Which they usually do, when I'm around.

I'm feeling guilty about missing church, about making Dad and the other kids miss it too, although the kids are probably grateful. I don't really know if church is my dad's big priority or if he's just making sure we get his precious car home. He didn't used to be so big on praying.

In the coolness of the kitchen, I shiver, whether from the cold or dread, I'm not sure.

Heading for the verandah, I look for a place to rest. No use doing anything more around here. Nobody will even notice and when they finally wake up, they'll no doubt just mess the place up again.

Why should I worry anyway? It's not *my* parent's place. As if we could afford a place at the lake.

I start thinking about the car. How, in our family, even a car is a luxury. We'd better not let anything happen to that car, that's all I can say.

Finding an old patchwork quilt thrown in the corner, I grab it and head for the big wicker rocker.

I pull my feet up and tuck them under my butt, wrap the old quilt around my shoulders and stare out at the lake. It's like glass this time of morning. By afternoon, it'll be all churned up by the boats, but right now, you can see the white sand beneath the water. You can feel the silence.

The sun is piercing my eyelids and a sweat bead breaks free, trickles down my upper lip, tickling me awake. Yawning, I look around. The place is deserted.

Now where's everyone? There's no sign of life at the cabin, but our car is still out back, so at least Katy hasn't buggered off to some other party without me.

I gather up our towels and bathing suits and walk out to the car. Maybe if I get everything ready, Katy will have enough sense to head for home as soon as she gets back. Dad can work up an awful head of steam if you give him the chance, and we're walking a pretty thin line as it is.

The plastic seat covers protecting the red velour upholstery are sticky in the heat, so I roll down all the windows.

Someone has set a beer on the Merc's hood and it's tipped over, beer washing down the front of the car and drying on the grill. I grab the bottle and set it on the porch steps.

Getting a rag from the kitchen, I go back out to the car and begin to rub the hood, trying to erase the beer stains, all the while checking the hood for scratches. Hopefully, the idiot who left his bottle at least made sure it wasn't sandy before he set it on my father's precious car.

The beer is dried in foamy streaks and I can smell the hops in the sun. If I can smell it, you can be sure my dad will too, so I sneak through the bushes to the cabin next door and grab a red plastic pail from the kid's sandbox.

I head for the lake, moving with great stealth. I imagine these were the folks who turned us in last night, so I don't suppose they'd look kindly on me stealing their kid's toys.

It takes me three trips to the shore and back before I'm satisfied. The car looks better than it did when we left the farm. Beer works real good for removing bugs.

It also seems to work well for removing brains, cause now it's 1:30 PM and still no sign of Katy.

I'm on the verandah, going through every pair of jeans I can find, looking for a dime to make another dreaded call home, when Katy and her group pull up in someone's rusted-out Chevy.

They come piling out of that old car like rabbits from a hat, and I wonder how they managed to get everyone in to start with. They head straight for the trunk and begin unloading vast quantities of beer.

"Katy, where have you been? Sometimes I think you don't have a brain in your head. Dad will be furious and we still haven't got any gas."

She flashes me a confident grin and as the last beer case is unloaded, I spot a red jerrycan at the back of the trunk.

"Here," she says, "I've been out getting the gas while you sleep like you don't have a worry in the world. So don't say I never help out."

And she waves toward the gas can as she heads to the verandah and grabs herself a cool one.

The can is heavy and I have trouble heaving it over the lip of the trunk. I'm in an awful rush, wanting to get on the road before Katy has time to drink more beer. One is okay and two is still fine, but getting her to come home anytime after number three will be damn near impossible.

I'm not sure I'll be able to accomplish my task within the two-beer time limit when I feel someone's hand on the heavy can, almost covering mine. I look up from my determined dragging, and there's Murray, looking at me and smiling his big lazy smile.

"Here, let me give you a hand. This can's way too heavy for a little girl like you to be hauling around all by yourself." And he lifts it like it's bone-dry and heads toward the car.

I'm so grateful I feel like crying. No one else has even noticed, they're all so intent on getting their first beer while it's still frosty.

Not that Murray doesn't like his beer too. Last night he tried to kiss me but he was so drunk he missed my mouth and ended up kissing my left cheekbone. I'm sure he doesn't even remember, but I do and I feel my face start to flush.

He empties the can into the gas tank and looks at me, smiling. "There, that should get the old girl back on the road." And he gives the fender a pat as he finishes screwing on the gas cap and throws the jerrycan into the backyard.

I notice the muscles bulging against the shoulder of his ripped T-shirt.

I feel the flush creep up my neck again. Darn this blushing! If I could just control it. But of course, I can't, not any better than I can control Katy.

"Okay, kiddo, just toss me the keys and we'll see if we can get her fired up. She was almost sucking air so it might take a pump or two. Gotta watch you don't flood 'er."

I hesitate, looking for Katy. She's sitting on a lawn chair down by the beach, using her lovely white teeth to twist the cap off yet another bottle of beer.

"Toss me those keys and let's see what happens."

I look at Murray, sitting impatiently in the driver's seat, but I don't toss him the keys, I walk around to the passenger side and get in. He flashes me a grin and brushes my palm lightly as he lifts the precious keys from my hand.

The old Merc starts first crack. That's one of the reasons my dad bought it.

It might not be a great beauty, but it's big, and reliable too. He's so damn proud of his car it's almost sad.

"Thanks a lot," I say, opening the door. "Can you tell Katy we're ready to roll? And thanks again."

But Murray has no intentions of leaving. He reaches across my body and pulls the door closed again while throwing the car in gear.

"Not so fast," he says as he guns the motor. "We might as well take her for a spin."

And he flips a U-ball out of the yard and onto the narrow gravel road, fishtailing like crazy.

He's started out too fast, and for one heart-stopping moment I think we're going to slide off the gravel and into an approach. But he eases off the gas and straightens her out at the last possible moment.

"Wanna do some ditch dipping?" he yells, over the sound of the wind whipping through the open windows. Now we're in and out of the ditches, still at breakneck speed.

"No, please, you've gotta stop!"

Tears are streaming down my face and drying instantly in the hot wind. "My dad will kill me. No one is supposed to drive this car. Please . . . "

He's holding the wheel lightly with one hand, seemingly unconcerned.

The ditches whirl around us, up and down. My stomach lurches every time the old Merc does and I hang onto the dashboard for dear life.

The waves of wheat lining the roadside are flying by in a blur as we top the rise onto the gravel road heading west toward the highway.

"Great, eh?" he asks, grinning.

"For God's sake, slow down!" I holler above the roar of the wind.

"Okay," he says, "I will, if you slide over a little closer," and he pats the seat beside him.

I'm terrified, so I slide over. As I do, he slows the car to normal speed and I begin to breathe again, my body sagging against his in relief.

Suddenly, he drops his arm, which he'd been resting on the top of the seat behind me and his hand grazes my breast.

I lean forward, fiddling with the radio, and ignore him. Maybe it was a mistake. After a few minutes I relax.

Next time he makes his move, there's no mistake as his oil-stained fingers slide down my breast.

I jerk from his touch, grabbing the wheel and giving him a good solid elbow at the same time.

He reacts by flooring the old Merc, wrestling the wheel from me as he holds down the gas. We slew wildly down the gravel leading to the intersection.

The approach to the highway is too steep, and as Murray tries to straighten the wheel, our tires lose contact with the ground. This time, we're airborne.

Murray is still steering, but it's having no affect. We haven't got an inch of ground left to work with. We hit the dirt with the wheel twisted sharply left and the old Merc just can't right herself. She begins a slow cartwheel, ungainly and awkward, like a two-ton ballerina.

Everything has slowed down, even my screaming. It seems endless in the hot afternoon. The car finally comes to a rest on its roof, having done a whole flip and part of another one.

I crawl from the wreckage, feeling like I've been on the working end of a jackhammer for a whole day.

Frantically, I look for Murray. I can't see him anywhere. Then I hear him groan and find him in the long grass, lying on his back, seemingly unhurt.

"Jesus," he says, shading his eyes and looking up at me. "Didn't know your old boat had the guts for a ride like that. Wanna help me up?"

I reach down to give him a hand, but stop halfway. Instead, I smack him, hard, leaving the rosy imprint of my hand on his cheek.

Kneeling, I straddle him, pushing my whole body weight into his belly.

"Take it easy, babe," he says, looking up at me. "You don't hafta flip out."

"You idiot," I holler, pushing harder against his ribcage. "You just wrecked my dad's car and you don't give a shit. Anything to cop a feel, right?"

His eyes are wide and I can feel his muscles knotting, his entire body tense.

"Okay, asshole," I say, "You're so interested, take a good look."

And I strip off my T-shirt, throwing it into the wind where it sails for a glorious moment before it hits the dust in the summerfallow behind me.

I undo the clasps of my bra. Dropping the straps, I toss it in the same general direction as the T-shirt.

Suddenly, Murray is deathly still beneath my body. I stare down at him and he turns his head away, closing his eyes.

"Chickenshit," I say, as I stand, spitting in the dust beside him.

I walk away, scanning the horizon, looking for Katy.

The Gift

Barbara Haworth

"You're too young to join up," barked the army officer. "Walk around the block and come back. You'll be another year older then."

And in the late summer sunshine of 1914, I ran around the Manchester recruiting office, went back in and found myself a soldier at age sixteen. I'm seventeen now, shivering with December cold and wet in a mud-filled trench in France overlooking a No Man's Land of stunted tree trunks, craters of mud, and stretches of barbed wire separating me from the enemy. I have forgotten colour; my eyes only know brown and grey now.

I'm scared all the time and half-formed prayers run nonstop through my head: *Please God . . . Don't let me die . . . Don't let my leg be blown to smithereens like my chum, Harry. Please God . . .* Strange that I'm praying, because I don't believe in God up here. None of us do, because we're in hell.

"Bert! Mail for you . . . "

I eagerly stretch out my hand to Ewan for the post from home. I had hoped for a Christmas parcel: toffee, cocoa, cigarettes, and dry socks. Oh, for dry socks. I know it's been sent, just delayed by the war, so I swallow my disappointment and tear open the envelope. These letters are my only contact to sanity: heat, food other than bully beef and hard-tack, my sister Mary's account of her factory work, my fourteen-year-old brother Stanley's adventures as a telegram boy and Mum's woeful tales of the shops and neighbours. I read the letters again and again until the paper is soft and worn.

Unfolding the letter, a picture falls out. I snatch the photograph before it disappears into the brown mire at the bottom of the trench and turn it over to see Mum, Mary and Stanley smiling at me. My chest suddenly feels so tight I think it'll burst. Why did I ever join this war I ask myself, as I do a dozen times a day, though I know the answer. Patriotic duty I had told Mum, standing before her kitted out in my crisp brown uniform, dismayed at the tears in her eyes. Mostly though, the promise of adventure and excitement made me join up. I was tired of the old sameness at home in Manchester: street, people, church and shops . . . sameness I now crave. Yes, adventure and the army's promise the war would be over by Christmas lured me, but here I am in a rain-slick trench, my great-coat soaked to my waist, my uniform in tatters, and it's Christmas Eve.

"Oh, Bert." Ewan is back from delivering the mail. "The colonel's looking for you." He scratches furiously under his arm. We're all lousy up here, the bugs burrowing into our wool clothing, and we stink, too, after days on duty without a bath or change of underwear.

I gather up my rifle and check the red band is around my upper sleeve showing I am the battalion runner, the person responsible for taking messages from unit to unit.

"I hear they're sending up a hot meal and plum pudding for Christmas dinner," Ewan says. "And bacon for breakfast."

"Sounds great," I tell him, as I tuck Mum, Mary and Stanley into the pocket of my coat and prepare to leave.

Ewan suddenly pushes himself straight and tilts his head, alert. "One's coming in!" he shouts.

The men around me stop chattering and listen hard. "To the right," someone yells and we all drop left as a shell whizzes over our heads and lands with a thud and explosion of mud and flame. When the smoke clears we see it has missed the trench, and us, though the force of the blast has collapsed part of the dirt and sand wall. Men rush immediately to shore it up again.

The trenches are dug to an average man's height and being short I don't need to crouch to run them to headquarters. As I slip and slide through mud, I remember standing in the food queue one grey dawn, the fellow in front of me tall, his head sticking out over the trench, and him suddenly falling down at my feet, a bullet from a sniper through his ear.

My mind on him instead of where I am going, my foot flies from underneath me and I fall headfirst into the muck. Several days of rain has churned everything into a thick, stinking mess and I am covered in it from head to toe. Men have been known to drown out here in this mud, especially if they hit a deep crater while running the narrow gap between ourselves and the Germans when we are ordered over the top. I pull myself up and wipe the worst of the grime off as best I can. I might have been uncomfortable before, but now I'm miserable. But I remind myself that I have not been dry from the knees down since I came to France so what's a little more wet. Besides I have a job to do.

A gun clatters half-heartedly from the other side of the barbed wire, and I automatically duck as I run. I often think I am lucky to be the battalion runner taking messages all over the trenches, because I never stand still in one place long enough to get hit. That's about the only reason I can think for why I am still alive when so many who came over with me are dead.

I reach headquarters and sit in a cubbyhole waiting for the colonel to finish his meeting in his office. I don't mind the wait as it is warm here, a small fire burning cheerily in a metal drum with a real kettle set on it, water bubbling for the colonel's tea. The walls of the office and this outer room are corrugated tin over dirt. A wood slat roof with more tin slapped over it keeps most of the weather out. I debate pulling my boots and socks off to try to dry my feet. They'd been tender lately and I knew a lot of the men had taken sick with sore feet, some even losing their toes to the damp, but the meeting ends, men file out of the office, then the colonel himself. He hands me a message.

"I need this taken to the Scottish boys," he says. "Seems headquarters is afraid the enemy may be contemplating an attack during Christmas hoping to catch us off guard. Want us to be extra vigilant."

I'm surprised he told me so much. I carry the messages, but I never know what is in them. Must be Christmas loosening his tongue.

The Colonel strokes his moustache thoughtfully. "Rotten time of year to be away from home, isn't it?" As if he read my mind.

To my horror I feel tears spring to my eyes. I try not to think of Mum, Mary and Stanley in my pocket.

The colonel grasps my shoulder. "No shame in missing family at Christmas," he says. "We'll get this mess straightened out over here and be home for the next one. Happy Christmas, Bert."

"Happy Christmas, Sir," I croak back.

Dark has fallen by now and the air holds the clarity of approaching deep cold. I splash through an ice-encrusted puddle, its broken shards gleaming as silver as the stars hanging low over the battered land. The Scottish boys, the 2nd Scots Guards, man the frontmost trenches, the German lines so close the men hear each other's voices on a still night, though they do not understand the words. It is such a narrow bit of land, yet neither us of can say we own it. I give the message to the company captain, then stop for a cigarette and a natter with a couple of the men.

It is eerily quiet, but I keep remembering the commander's words that an attack could come at any time, and my nerves feel jangled. My breath puffs white and my damp pant legs become stiff with cold.

"Well, look at that." Cautiously peering over the trench top, a soldier points across No Man's Land.

Carefully, we poke our heads over the dirt wall, always aware a sniper's bullet might be waiting for us. Things stay quiet and we get braver and stand upright. From the other side of barbed wired we see pinpoints of yellow light.

"Christmas trees," the first man whispers. "The Germans have real Christmas trees lit with candles in their trenches. Now where do you think they got those?"

Stretching to my full length, I see more lights wink all along the enemy line. I catch my breath at this wondrous magic in so barren a place. The sound of singing suddenly swells — "Silent Night" recognized though sung in its native tongue. We give them, "O Little Town of Bethlehem" in return. As I sing the carol I've only before sung in a church, I cannot stop the strangeness of it all, the singing of Bethlehem and Christ's birth and peace with both our and the German dead lying in frozen lumps on the ground between us. We put all caution aside and scramble from the trenches, walking freely in the new knowledge there will not be an attack tonight.

After a while, I decide to return to my own unit and begin to run the trenches, then suddenly I am lost. In the dark. I, who know every twist and turn of every trench, don't know where I am. A white fog rises from the frozen ground, wrapping me in thick, curling strands and I stand frozen with fear — if I go that way will I find myself in enemy lines? I jump nervously as something bumps into my foot — a rat. I'll have to stay here until daybreak, I decide.

I hollow a hole in the trench wall and climb in, folding into myself for warmth, but the cold seeps into my bones until my teeth chatter. I'll have to move if I don't want frostbite. I slip from my shelter and jump up and down, thumping my arms against my thighs to get warm. What a Christmas Eve, I tell myself, and once again I'm fighting back tears. They're not that far away, Mum, Mary and Stanley. Just over the water in England, a day's travel. Then suddenly I know I am never seeing them again. I'll die out here from cold or illness or bullets or shrapnel.

Unexpectedly, I hear weeping nearby. At first I think it myself, then realize it is coming from further down the trench. Holding my rifle at ready, I creep along, then stop and listen. The crying sounds nearer. I crouch low and hug the dirt wall and stumble over a man, head in his hands, sobbing. I see the gleam of a bayonet, the dark grey uniform and metal helmet — a German! The enemy. I clutch my rifle tightly and sweat trickles down my back, but he merely looks up, makes a half-hearted move towards his weapon, then sinks his chin to his chest again. I've never seen a German soldier before. We shoot and bombard a faceless enemy. White flutters from his hand. I light a match and pick up the paper to see I hold a picture of a man, woman and a small boy.

"Your family?" I ask.

I light another match and hold it to his face, not sure if he understands me. I dig in my pocket and take out my photograph of Mum, Mary and Stanley and hold it out to him. He glances at it and raises a tear-stained face to search my own.

With shock I stare at a clean-shaven chin that has never seen a razor and realize this boy is more Stanley's age than mine. He is muddy, shivering, scared and desperately homesick, his eyes saying everything my heart has been telling me all day. He buries his head in his hands again, shoulders shaking. "Mutter," I think I hear him whisper.

I do the only thing I can think of. I set aside my rifle, crowd into the hole next to the boy and put my arms around him.

Christmas morning stretches pink and grey above a white blanket of ground-hugging fog as I wake to find I am alone. My picture is tucked carefully in my pocket along with a thick pair of wool socks. The sun quickly burns the mist away and I know where I am. I chide myself for my foolishness in becoming so easily confused, then soon find my company and enjoy bacon and biscuits and hot tea for breakfast. We stand and stretch unafraid, as up and down the line an unplanned Christmas truce between German and English takes place. I won't die today. The chaplain leads us in Christmas services, and we sing carols and smoke cigarettes courtesy of Queen Mary and King George. We light a huge fire and I pull off my boots and wet socks and set them next to it to dry. I feel a moment of concern to see my toenails so black, but soon my feet are dry and pink and I put the fresh socks on.

"Where'd you get those?" Ewan asks.

"Christmas gift," I tell him.

The Catalyst

Jocelyn Shipley

You're a girl who's good at science. You're such a geek you don't even try to hide it. You love the smell of a lab and the look of all that equipment: beakers, test tubes, clamps and stands. You love knowing scientific terms, like collision theory, activation energy, catalyst. You are happiest with your textbook open, apparatus ready, about to begin an experiment.

Your chemistry teacher, Ms. Bonelli, recommends you for a special summer program where you spend a month at a university messing around with technology. It's your dream come true and you adore her. But two weeks later, she ruins your life. When you walk into class, there's a new student in your lab partner Kate's place. Kate, who you hope is sort of your friend, is sitting way across the room.

The new person doesn't speak. Her round face looks blank. She's chewing gum, slowly, like she can't be bothered, then every so often giving the wad a rude snap. She's short and plump and pale, a mushroom sprouting on the lab stool. You're tall and bony, more like an overgrown thistle.

"Alexis," Ms. Bonelli says after class, "I put Rochelle beside you because I hope you can help her. She's trying to finish high school; she dropped out a few years back."

You don't say anything, in case you start to scream. It isn't fair. You want to sit with Kate, you were just getting to know her, you were just getting accepted by her group. Your parents would say: Stand up for your rights, don't let anybody push you around. But not in this case. In this case they'd say: What a great chance to help someone less advantaged than yourself. Go for it.

"Please try, Alexis," Ms. Bonelli says. "Rochelle's scared she can't do it. It took a lot of courage for her to come back. You're the only one both smart and patient enough to help her." You know why Ms. Bonelli says this. She's met your do-goody social-worker parents, who would say: Think of helping Rochelle this way. She's trying an experiment. She wants to see if she can get her chemistry credit. You can be the catalyst. You can make it easier for her.

At lunch you sit with Kate and her friends. As you admire and wish for their perfect outfits, you realize you don't want to be a catalyst. You want to be Kate. You also realize Kate's told them about chemistry class. Everybody's laughing. "Hey, watch you don't catch it," they say. "Yeah, Lexi, look out, it might be contagious."

You look as vacant as Rochelle did in class. "Catch what?" Then they're all quiet, looking around at each other and rolling their eyes. You'd like to smack them, but you just say, "What do you mean?"

"Alexis," Kate says, patting your arm as if you were three years old, "didn't you notice your new friend Rochelle's pregnant?"

You realize with a throw-up kind of feeling it's not Rochelle they're laughing at. It's you. You, the girl who memorized the periodic table for fun. The girl who's never had a boyfriend. The girl who's never even kissed anybody yet.

The next day you think about skipping chemistry. Say for the rest of the term. How long could you get away with it? Or maybe you could drop the course. But you're not just taking it because you have to, like most kids. When you were little, your favourite activity was mixing potions. Your parents gave you baking soda and vinegar and food colouring, stuff like that to play with. Your best birthday present ever was your first chemistry set.

You remember about that summer program. To get accepted, you have to have high marks, but you also have to show leadership skills. You decide to at least look like you're trying. You walk in and smile at Rochelle. "Hi," you say, "I'm Alexis."

Rochelle blows a bubble. "Can I copy your homework?"

"Um," you say. You don't know what to do. You always let Kate copy, but only because you know she could do the work if she ever bothered. "Um, you didn't do it?"

"Nah, too hard. Anyways, *Crazy for Cash* was on last night."

Ms. Bonelli is watching you. "Well, maybe I could help you with it? Like after school or something?" You can't look Rochelle in the eye, so you stare at her necklace instead. You've never seen anything like it. It's made of the usual wire and beads, but in between are bits of hardware, things like nuts and bolts and screws.

Rochelle shifts on the stool, tugs at her long grey sweat-shirt. "Nah, forget it." The word BABY is printed across her full breasts and a big red arrow points down at her bulging belly. "I gotta get home right away, like."

At lunch Kate and her friends are still teasing you from yesterday.

"Hey brainer, where do babies come from?"

"Duh, Lexi thinks the stork brings them."

"No she doesn't, she thinks you make them in test tubes."

"Ha, ha," you say, as if you are one of them. As if everything you know about sex didn't come from a book. As if you are a woman of experience. So hip, so cool.

Then you notice Rochelle sitting in a corner, all by herself. You look away. But you know how it feels to sit alone and you can't block her out. Nor can you block out the image your parents and Ms. Bonelli are sending to your brain. All you can see is a fresh page in your chemistry notebook, with this equation:

Rochelle + Hard Work ——>Chemistry credit.

Your name is written over the arrow, as the catalyst.

"Lexi," Kate says, "can I borrow your chem notes tonight? I should get caught up, in case smelly-Bonelli checks our books."

You don't answer right away. Then suddenly you are standing up. "I don't think so," you say. "I promised them to Rochelle." For once there is absolute silence at the table. As you leave you feel like you're walking on that black arrow. You can hear Kate and her group's speechlessness all the way to Rochelle's corner.

"Is anybody sitting here?" you ask.

She smiles. "I don't see nobody."

You sit. You open your lunch bag but you don't feel like eating.

"Hey," Rochelle says, "got anything you don't want? God, I'm starving."

"Yeah, sure. Bagel with cream cheese? Apple?"

"No chips? No chocolate? I get these terrible cravings."

"Sorry."

"That's okay, not good for the baby anyways."

"When are you, um — "

"Due, like? June 24. Hoping for a boy, this time."

"This time?"

"Yeah, I already got a little girl, Shareen. She's two. That's why I dropped out last time, see, and got married, and that's why I gotta get home. Brady watches her all day, then when I come back is when he can work."

"Oh. What's his job?"

"Fixes things, CD players and VCRs and that, at home."

"What made you come back to school?"

"Well see, me and Brady, we're trying to make a better life for our kids. I wanna get into nursing, that's why I gotta get chemistry."

After that you help Rochelle as much as you can. You don't tell your parents; they'd be far too proud. But you can't hide it from Kate. "You're so good to her," Kate says. "I mean, I couldn't do it. You're such a nice person, Lexi."

"No, I'm not," you say. "I'm just a catalyst."

"A what?" Kate says. "God, don't talk like that, no one will ever go out with you." She swats the side of your head.

"But hey, could you ask her where she got that cool necklace?"

"She made it," you say. "She uses stuff from her husband's workshop."

"Would she make me one?" Kate wants to know. "I'll pay her whatever."

"Dunno," you say. You remember the day you hinted to Rochelle that you'd like a necklace like hers, but she just said how busy she was with her kid and chemistry. You promise Kate you'll ask, but you've no intention of doing so. Even though you know Rochelle could use the money, you don't want Kate wearing one of her necklaces. They're far too special.

Ms. Bonelli notices how hard you're trying with Rochelle. Often, on the way out of class, she says quietly, "Thank you, Alexis." Then one day she tells you you've been accepted into that summer program. But you don't even care anymore. It's like the rest of the world doesn't exist. All you want is for Rochelle to get her credit.

It's not easy being a catalyst though. When you explain how to write up an experiment, she usually says, "Nah, it's too hard for me, I'm just too stupid." Or maybe, "I'm too tired, Shareen was up all bloody night." And she's not much of a lab partner. She breaks a beaker and a test tube and almost explodes the Bunsen burner.

But you don't give up. After all, you are part of a chemical reaction now. You have collided with Rochelle, and activated her. Now you must produce results.

And then, after Spring Break, Rochelle stops coming to school. A day, a week, a month. "I don't think she's coming back," Ms. Bonelli tells you. "She has so much else to deal with."

You don't know what to do. You should be glad; it's a whole lot easier, just doing all the labs by yourself. But you miss Rochelle. You miss being part of her equation. You wonder how she's doing. You wonder what happened.

You can't call her; she doesn't have a phone. But you know where she lives. So one day you cram your chemistry textbook and notes into your backpack and head out there after school. The weather is mild, the snow all melted, and you jog like you're training for track. Until you pass the plaza. Then you're in the north side of town, where Rochelle's street is. You slow down.

You're in a subdivision of semi-detached bungalows that could all use painting. The air has that spring smell of wet dog. You remember the article in the local paper about all the illegal basement apartments here. People say they should be banned because they don't have two exits. Recently a woman and her three kids died in a fire.

"But the rent's cheap," Rochelle has told you. "It's the only place we can afford."

You find Rochelle's house and knock at the side door. Nothing happens so you knock again. And again.

After a long time, Rochelle appears. She looks dazed. "Sorry, I was laying down," she says. Her hair is messy and she's not wearing her usual makeup. She looks a whole lot younger than twenty-one. She also looks huge, as if she's about to give birth any minute. A little thumb-sucking kid is attached to her leg. They take up the whole doorway.

"Hi," you say. "Hi Rochelle." You shift your backpack from one shoulder to the other. "Is this Shareen? She's so cute."

Rochelle grins. "Yeah, this is Shareen, the little bugger, she's been driving me crazy today." Her arm goes around the kid, hugging the fuzzy head to her thigh. "Hey, I hope you didn't bring me no homework, 'cause I dropped out again, eh?"

You stand there feeling like an even bigger geek than you are. "Oh no," you say, "I just . . . " Somehow you didn't really plan what to say. You kind of figured Rochelle would want to get right down to work.

Shareen looks up at you with big dark eyes. Her hair is full of barrettes, pink, yellow and blue, shaped like bears and butterflies and flowers. "I like your hair," you sort of whisper to her.

"Well, c'mon in," Rochelle says.

You follow her down the stairs, into the aroma of Kraft Dinner and stale smoke. She's told you about her apartment but you're still surprised how small it is. There's just a bedroom and a bathroom and the kitchen. Just a table and a sofa and a TV, which is on top volume at a soap. Tools and wires and old, broken electronic things are heaped in a corner. There aren't any windows.

"Have a pop?" Rochelle says. She takes out two cans and hands Shareen a baby bottle of apple juice.

You can't help seeing there's not much else in the fridge. "Oh, no thanks, that's okay, just water's fine. I walked over."

"Why?" Rochelle says. You know she doesn't mean why'd you walk. She wants to know why you're here. So do you.

"I was wondering," you say, sitting down at the table, "if you're coming back? Ms. Bonelli said not, but I wish you would. I mean, just a couple more months and you'd be finished, you'd have the credit."

Shareen brings a ratty-looking stuffed bear from the sofa and plops it onto your lap. "Hey, thanks," you say. She just stares at you, sucking on her bottle of juice. Then she stares at the TV.

Rochelle sits down at the table too, wincing as if it hurts. "God, my back," she says, "it's brutal. No, I'm not coming back to school. Brady got a job, see, working days, and I gotta look after Shareen now."

"Well," you say, "what about going to Deacon High? Don't they have a daycare?"

Rochelle slumps over the table, her head on her arms. "Look, I'm just too tired, okay? All I wanna do is eat and sleep and play with Shareen. I can't study."

"But I could help you. I could tutor you."

"Yeah sure, we already tried that. And I flunked the friggin' mid-term, remember?"

"Not by much though." You feel like your mother. You say, "Oh please, give it another try," and then you sound like your mother too.

Rochelle straightens and stretches, looks at you as if you just landed from Mars. "I'm not giving up," she says. "I'm just taking a break for a bit." She sets down her pop and lifts Shareen onto her lap, shifting her shape until she can hold the child comfortably.

Shareen tugs at Rochelle's necklace, one you haven't seen before. It's even funkier than the others. Less beads, more hardware.

"Don't break Mommy's necklace now, Share," Rochelle says. She lifts Shareen's hand off and gives it a quick kiss. "Hey, guess what? I sold some of my necklaces down at the plant where Brady works. Everybody's asking for them. I'm gonna start making bracelets and anklets too."

"That's terrific!" you say. "And you could sell them at school, you know, when you come back."

Rochelle makes a face. "Yeah, right. Hey, I almost forgot." She slides Shareen off her lap and waddles into the bedroom. When she returns she's holding out a necklace to you. "I made this for ya," she says, "to thank you for all your help. Don't think I don't appreciate it."

"Oh my god," is all you can say. Besides the bits of hardware, your necklace is strung with beads the colour of copper sulfate, which you've told Rochelle is your favourite. "I love it," you cry. "I absolutely love it, thank you so much." You put the necklace on and ask, "What are the tiny silver things called, anyway?"

"Nuts," Rochelle says. "Cap nuts and hex nuts and wing nuts."

"Nuts, Mommy?" Shareen says. "Can we have some peanuts?"

Rochelle laughs and hugs her. "Hey, that really cracks me up," she says. And then, nodding at the necklace, "Looks good, Lexi."

You feel like you might start to cry. You observe that you are not the catalyst here. You can't be, you conclude, because things look so different to you now than before you met Rochelle. And being a girl who's good at science, you know that the catalyst in a reaction doesn't undergo any change.

You must look like you're going to cry, because Rochelle says, "Don't worry, I'll go back to school sometime, for something that don't need science. Maybe get my early childhood ed. I'm good with kids."

"Okay," you say. "Well, let me know when you have the baby. I'll come see you in the hospital."

"Sure," Rochelle says. "I'll do that."

You know she won't though. You'll probably never meet again.

Or if you do, say at the movies or up at the mall, you'll both just say, "Hey, how's it going?" You'll say how sweet Rochelle's kids are and she'll ask if you got your Ph.D. yet. Then you'll both sort of smile and say, "Well, gotta go now, good to see ya."

Dog

Jean Rand MacEwen

The dog and the man made their slow, painful way through back alleys and lanes checking garbage bins, bags and dumpsters. The dog knew the route as well as the man. Both knew where there were good pickings, except that on this cold Friday there was not much to pick. Both were hungry. When the man found a half-eaten hamburger he divided it meticulously, and they ate together. They lingered near the art school. Students often tossed away perfectly good food.

"Hey, neat dog."

Hearing his name dog looked up, raised his pointed ears and eyed the girl hopefully. She was eating a hot dog.

"What's his name?"

"Just Dog."

"Hello, Dog. Can I draw you?"

Dog wagged his tail, his longing eyes on the hot dog.

"I think he likes me."

The old man shrugged. The girl shifted her backpack around, set it on a snowbank and took out a sketch pad. She worked quickly, and suddenly — there was Dog, one ear up, the other down, his grizzled muzzle, his shaggy, matted fur.

A group of students stopped to chat, to look, and to critique the charcoal drawing.

"Not bad — not bad at all. You'd better hand that in for your assignment. You've really got him, that scruffy black and grey, that muddy fur."

"Cheap model," said another student. "What are you going to pay him?"

The young artist looked at Dog. "How about half a cold hot dog?"

Dog understood, wagged his tail furiously and accepted the hot dog. He devoured it in one bite.

"Thanks, Mister. Nice dog," said the artist as the students moved away.

Dog looked up at the man. Gnarled fingers scratched behind his ears. Dog liked this.

"Old Greedy-guts, I shared with you. But I guess you're skinnier than I am."

The old man coughed and the two moved on.

As the cold intensified the man decided to seek shelter for the night. If he went early he might find them a place together. He tried every place he could think of — the mission, the lighthouse — but the answer was always the same. "You know we can't take in a dog." Finally he gave up.

Man and Dog moved through the darkening city making their way over to Yonge Street. Here they had a bit of luck. Someone tossed a Styrofoam take-out carton onto the road. The man scrambled for it. Rice. There must have been chicken on top because there was a lingering taste. And it was hot, or at least warm. The two shared the meal.

Their luck held. A grating over the subway was not occupied. They spent the bitter night with their two cold bodies pressed together for a little warmth and comfort. Dog was disturbed by the man's constant coughing, and gently he licked the grimy face, pressing his body still closer to the man's chest. They shivered together.

Long before the gray winter dawn crept into the city the man and the dog prepared to leave the subway grating. Dog was stiff and sore. He held his left hind foot off the cold sidewalk. The man rubbed his swollen knees and sighed. Dog let him look at the sore foot. It felt good when the man blew his warm breath on it but another coughing spell put an end to that bit of comfort.

The day passed much like any other day except that both Man and Dog were noticeably weaker. For a while they found shelter in a doorway, but it was no protection from the penetrating cold. As they huddled together, their bodies pressed close, the man eased his cold fingers into Dog's fur.

"Dog," he said, "you are just bones and fur. We'll neither of us come through another night on the street."

Painfully he got to his feet.

"Come Dog," he wheezed. The two started limping east. Dog walked with his head hanging low, his tail between his legs, but never for a moment did he leave the man.

When at last they entered a building Dog was suddenly nervous. The warmth was nice but the smell — that awful smell. The smell of fear. Another animal had been frightened here, in this place. He pressed himself against the man's legs trembling and unhappy. The gnarled hand stroked his head but Dog was not reassured.

As the man eased up to the desk he knew that the woman behind it smelled their approach and tried, unsuccessfully, to hide her distaste. The man waited for her to speak.

"Yes?"

"Needs a home," said the man indicating Dog. Dog whimpered as if to reinforce the idea.

The woman picked up a form.

"Name?"

"Dog."

"Yes, but what is the dog's name?" She put a kleenex to her nose.

"Dog. Just Dog." Hearing his name, Dog made an attempt to wag his tail.

"Owner?"

The man didn't answer. He wanted to take as long as possible. The warmth of the room made his feet and hands prickle and ache but he knew he needed to warm up. He also knew that the woman wanted to finish with him as soon as possible. He no longer smelled either himself or Dog but he knew they both must stink abominably.

"Who owns the dog?" Still no answer. "Who does the dog belong to?"

"Dog? He belongs to himself."

"I'll put down stray. You want to leave him here?"

The man was seized with a fit of coughing and shaking. His eyes ran. His nose ran.

The woman handed him the box of kleenex. "Keep the box," she said softly. "We'll look after Dog. He'll have a good meal, a bath and a nice cage to sleep in."

The man nodded. As he headed for the door Dog stood to follow as usual. An attendant slipped a collar around his neck and restrained him.

Dog howled, a long mournful howl. It was amazing how such a frail creature could produce such a volume of sound.

"Don't worry. He'll be alright after you have gone," she said kindly. "He'll be well looked after here."

Dog continued to cry long after his man was gone. He was too unhappy to eat more than a few bites of the meal provided. He submitted docilely to the medical examination and the washing.

"Will you look at that," said the girl with the soap. "He has a beautiful white ruff. He's a real dear. I hope we can save him."

"There are no basic problems," said the vet, "except that he is old and undernourished."

Two days later Dog was still not eating properly.

"He's been an outdoor dog. Perhaps," said the vet, "he'll respond to fresh air and exercise. He's so quiet and docile the new dog walker can take him."

Dog drooped along with the girl until they reached Queen Street. Suddenly he came alive. He knew where he was and he knew what he wanted. When they waited for a light to change Dog drew back his head, pulled with all his strength, and he was free. Free.

Dog was free and he knew where he was going. Dodging the traffic and hiding between parked cars, Dog eluded the dog walker and headed west.

He lacked the strength to keep up the original fast pace and reduced his run to a trot, then to a slow walk, but always he kept going west. At last he came to the area he knew. He checked all the familiar places, not for food but for his man. The man was not there. When Dog came to the Art School he slowed, hoping to find his man.

A student bent to pat him. "Hello, you." Dog wagged his tail. "That dog looks a bit like the one you drew."

The girl looked closely. "It is the same dog. I hardly recognized him. Someone's given him a bath. So, Dog," she said, "You earned me an A+. Are you hungry?"

Dog looked up hopefully. He could smell the wonderful aroma coming from the large box she was carrying.

"Come on, Dog." She opened a door. Dog didn't like buildings. He hesitated. "Come on. If you want to share my pizza you've got to come in. Its too bloody cold to stand around outside." When they had finished the pizza Dog was glad to sleep in the warm spot she found for him.

Late in the afternoon Dog heard, "Come on, Dog," and got to his feet. He stood on his hind legs with his front paws on her knees. He licked her hand.

When the door opened Dog took off. Rested and still full of pizza he set off at a good trot, heading east on Queen Street. Maybe his man was still near the place with the smell.

Without going too near the big red brick building Dog searched. Disconsolately he started down a little hill that led under the Queen Street bridge. He paused at the foot of a snowy embankment. With a little yip of excitement Dog picked up the familiar smell of his man.

Up the bank and behind some bushes Dog found him. The man had made a sort of nest in the snow, and covered with newspapers, he was dozing. Dog jumped on him yapping with joy. The man sat up coughing and annoyed

"Get away. Get away," he wheezed. Dog was not discouraged. He licked the familiar face.

"Oh Dog! Its you! I didn't recognize you. All that clean fluffy fur." He hugged the animal to his chest. "Oh, Dog," was all he said.

The old man shifted his position and coughed. He couldn't feel his feet at all but he eased his cold hands into Dog's fur. He had not intended to fall asleep. The sun, lowering in the west, had been shining feebly giving an illusion of warmth when he had dozed off, too weary to seek shelter in the places available to people like him. He rested his head on Dog's warm shoulder. Dog pressed against him and licked his face. The old man sighed. It was too late and he was too tired to try the Salvation Army or any of the other places. Besides he couldn't leave Dog. He rummaged in his pocket for the old banana he had been saving for morning. Both man and dog ignored the fact that it was mostly rotting mush.

The man tried to rearrange the newspapers to cover both himself and Dog. The exertion started another spell of violent coughing, and he gave up. Hugging Dog close to his aching chest the man dozed again.

Dog didn't notice as the wheezing slowed, but when it stopped altogether he roused to reach out and lick the cold cheek. There was no response.

Dog raised his head and howled, and howled again. Then lying on top of the man he rested his head between his outstretched paws, his nose against the man's chin.

THE TORONTO STAR
Wednesday, December 9 1999

MAN DIES IN THE RAVINE

Last night an unidentified man
and a dog froze to death under
the Queen Street bridge.

AGMV Marquis

MEMBER OF THE SCABRINI GROUP

Quebec, Canada
2001